The Garcia Family

Iva-Marie Palmer

GABBY GARCIA'S GARCIA'S

ULTIMATE PLAYBOOK

Illustrations by Marta Kissi

 KATHERINE TEGEN BOOKS
An Imprint of HarperCollins Publishers

Katherine Tegen Books is an imprint of HarperCollins Publishers.

Gabby Garcia's Ultimate Playbook

ISBN 978-0-06-239180-3

Typography by Katie Fitch
17 18 19 20 21   CG/LSCH   10 9 8 7 6 5 4 3 2 1
❖
First Edition

To my home team—Steve, Clark, and Nate

Hey, who are you?

Or, better question, who do you think you are, opening this extra-special possession of mine?

If this is Peter, put this book down. **NOW.**

If you're a good-hearted stranger who happened to find this because I somehow dropped it, well, I don't totally believe you because I don't totally believe that I would drop something as important as this.

But I'll give you the benefit of the doubt.

Maybe you think you hold in your hands a mere diary. But it's not that. **NOT A DIARY** at all.

Yeah, I know you're thinking, kid, this is 10,000% a diary. And what's wrong with diaries anyway?

Look: nothing is wrong with diaries. My stepmom has kept one since forever and she and my dad pretty much tie for top non-famous personal heroes.

But this, dear unauthorized reader (or should I say intruder?), is a play-book. **MY** ultimate playbook, in case you wanted clarification. It's where I keep all my thoughts and ideas and strategies about how to **WIN** at life.

Yeah, but how is that different from a diary, you ask?

Look, diaries are usually just about what happens.

Playbooks are about how you make things happen.

In sports, playbooks contain highly confidential plans that the opposing team can use to sabotage your game. Which is why I have to be highly suspicious of you because maybe you're someone who doesn't want me to win at life . . . like Mario Salamida, for example.

(Look, Mario, I can't help you've never gotten a hit off me. Go take some batting practice.)

There's also another difference between this and a diary. In diaries, people write about what happened to them and how it made them feel. Which is great. I love feelings. Like the feeling I get when I throw a fastball over home plate and watch as the batter swings and misses. There is no feeling better than that, **IMO**.

But playbooks are about Goals and Actions and Results. Deciding to do A in order to achieve B so the world can C how awesome you are. Haha. Playbooks contain rules and stuff that every great player can use to become **THE GREATEST OF ALL TIME**.

Nod if you've read and understood the signs, as all-star pitchers like me do.

Great. **NOW GO BURN THIS BOOK SO NO ONE CAN STEAL MY PLAYS!!!!**

(But don't really burn it. Do the nice thing and mail it back to me. I'll have my dad bake you some cookies.)

LINEUP AS OF PREGAME

GABRIELLE "GABBY" GARCIA (aka ME)

Height: 4'9" (hoping for a growth spurt)

Build: Wiry but strong enough to put a wicked spin on my fastball

Sport: Baseball, mainly, but I'm up for anything

Excels at: Pitching, observing opponents

Favorite Athlete: I refuse to pick just one

Motto: "The main thing is to care. Care very hard, even if it is only a game you are playing." —Billie Jean King, one of the greatest female tennis players ever

JUAN GARCIA (aka Dad)

JUAN GARCIA

(a.k.a. DAD)

Height: Something he calls "tall enough"

Build: Something he calls "huggable"

Sport: Likes all, plays anything he's invited to

Excels at: Writing, reading, cooking, doing things at the last minute

Favorite Athletes: Me and my brother, Peter (but I think it's Michael Jordan)

Motto: "Needs more hot sauce." (Plus a bunch of smart things said by dead people)

♡ LUPITA "LOUIE" GARCIA (aka my stepmom)

LUPITA 'LOUIE' GARCIA

(a.k.a. MY STEPMOM)

Height: Same as Oprah (she's very proud of this)

Build: Good enough for Oprah (she's very proud of this, too)

Sport: Yoga (but only the easy stuff, as she'd say)

Excels at: Management, math, getting things done

Favorite Athletes: Also me and my brother, Peter

Motto: "We can do it." —Rosie the Riveter

PETER GARCIA (aka my half brother)

Height: 4'9". Not happy to note that at eight he is as tall as me, his twelve-year-old sister.

Build: You can never gauge the full weight of a nuisance

Sport: Says soccer, but I think his true annoying talent is for smirking at things I say

Excels at: Driving me completely nuts

Favorite Athlete: Carli Lloyd, Olympic gold medal-winning soccer player (can't say he doesn't have good taste)

Motto: "Is this annoying?" "What about this?"

DIEGO PARKER (aka best friend, sort of sidelined due to being in Costa Rica—unbelievable that he's gone instead of here as my support system during this tumultuous time!)

DIEGO PARKER

(a.k.a. MY BEST FRIEND)

SIDELINED DUE TO BEING IN COSTA RICA

Height: Always too tall for his pants. TALL.

Build: String bean

Sport: Knowing everything about every sport in the known universe, plus probably some sports played on other planets

Excels at: Being light enough to carry off the field when he trips and falls. So he has said.

Favorite Athlete: Gabby Garcia (but in truth, I think Diego's fave is Yan Gustader, a hornussen player from Switzerland)

Motto: "All I want to do is go the distance." —Rocky (a character from an ancient movie our dads love)

MARIO SALAMIDA

(a.k.a. MY CLOSEST THING TO A MORTAL ENEMY)

MARIO SALAMIDA
(aka my closest thing to a mortal enemy)

Height: Tall enough to cast a scary shadow

Build: See above

Sport: Baseball

Excels at: First base, big hits, snarling, intimidation

6

Favorite Athlete: Definitely not me

Motto: A series of grunts and kicking things when games don't go his way

April 10
How I Got Here: A Replay

Okay, so this is my playbook. But I'm starting with a replay. Which maybe makes this a little like a diary, and I just wrote that whole note about how it's **NOT A DIARY**. Replays are different, though.

I'll need it, for the sake of context and historical posterity and stuff. Because what I'm writing here is the reason for me starting this playbook in the first place.

Anyway . . . it was the perfect day for a baseball game. Blue sky, green grass, birds chirping so it almost sounds like they're singing the national anthem but without messing up any high notes.

Everyone I know and love—plus my irritating little brother, Peter—was in the stands, cheering me on.

As they should have been because I was pitching the **BEST GAME OF MY LIFE**.

The **BEST GAME OF MY LIFE IN THE BEST SEASON OF MY LIFE**.

My capital letters are completely justified.

Leading up to that point, it had been a record-setting year.

As a Luther Junior High 7th grader, I had straight As for the first time. My best friend, Diego, and I got along with everyone in my class. My braces had just come off and my yearbook photo was my best one of my lifetime. I had **ZERO** weird middle-school moments with mean girls and bullies. Also, at some point after Christmas break, my ponytail stopped doing this stupid thing that made it look like I had a hairy shark fin on top of my head.

Furthermore, I was the starting pitcher/"Golden Child" of the Luther Lions, home team of Luther Junior High in Peach Tree, Georgia. (And I just want to tell my much older self, fondly looking back and reading this, that the "Golden Child" nickname came from my Luther coach. **AND COACHES ARE ALWAYS RIGHT.**)

OTHER AMAZING THINGS THAT HAPPEN WHEN YOU ARE GOLDEN CHILD

- The *Peachtree Gazette* ran a full-color picture on its front page of me pitching.

- The cafeteria ladies gave me extra french fries on French Fry Friday.

- My locker combination was 19 (my jersey number)–32 (the number of Sandy Koufax, a super-awesome pitcher from the 1960s)–11 (the number of Mo'ne Davis, my hero and the first girl pitcher to win a game in the Little League World Series)—and I hadn't screwed it up **ONCE.**

- I'd been invited to **EVERY** birthday party and pool party thrown by a seventh grader plus three pizza parties thrown by eighth graders who were on the baseball team.

- My team always gave me first pick of bus seats when we went to away games (I liked the one right in the middle of the bus so I could be in the **MIDDLE OF THE ACTION**).

- My coach had said if we went to regionals—which we would—we'd get to go to an Atlanta Braves game and have a congratulatory message on the **SCOREBOARD.**

I could go on, but the list would be too big and I need to get to the important stuff. And what's important is that I spell it out officially: I was on an entire-life win streak. Nothing could go wrong.

Except I was totally wrong about that.

Back to the replay. It was the top of the eighth and I was close to pitching a no-hitter.

(In case Old Me is *so* old I've forgotten a few key things about baseball, I'll explain.) A no-hitter is basically a unicorn for baseball. They are rarely seen and very prized. (Okay, so maybe no-hitters are more common than unicorns, but still they are **VERY. RARE.**)

My cheering section—yes, I had a **CHEERING SECTION**— was hooting and hollering and woo-wooing exactly how I liked it: they made lots and lots of noise until the moment just before I went into my windup, and then they gave me perfect silence so I could throw the perfect pitch. **PERFECTION** is a theme here.

So, yes, as I got ready to throw a curve, all eyes were on me as the fans in the stands went from their enthusiastic cheering into a quiet, awe-inspired trance. Hushed suspense, just like in a major league game. Except for a few chirping birds. Birds don't know any better.

It was just like they would have been if they suddenly saw a unicorn.

So there I was, on the mound, about to toss what was sure to be another strike to Andrew Herman, the best batter on the Archer Archers (really their team name, in case you're wondering, Old Me).

I gave myself a few seconds to soak up that feeling of something amazing about to happen. About to happen because I was going to *make it happen.*

I was going to strike Andrew out, and then in the 9th, the Archers' worst batters would come up. My plan was to get them out—one, two, three—end the game, secure the win.

A unicorn.

(Which would have been my second one for the season. **THE BEST SEASON OF MY LIFE. TWO UNICORNS.**)

So, if I had to make a rule for what you **DON'T** do when someone is about to pitch a no-hitter, it would be:

DON'T INTERRUPT!

But, if you're Dr. Simpkins, Luther Junior High's principal, you definitely interrupt.

Just as I was going into my windup, with the hushed crowd and everything, he came running onto the field. Oh, and then he yelled that everyone had to evacuate immediately.

And then I said, "Are you nuts???" It just came out of my mouth.

But no one heard me.

Because five guys in white jumpsuits came out of the school dressed like some kind of spacemen (or **UNICORN KILLERS**) and stood behind Dr. Simpkins.

"Hey, everybody," Dr. Simpkins hollered into the stands, which were no longer suspensefully quiet because once the principal told everyone they needed to go away, well, people started to **FREAK**. Andrew even put his bat down. Truly, it was like he had no respect I was about to strike him out!

Then Dr. Simpkins brought out a megaphone. "We're clearing the field and the school. We've just discovered a severe asbestos situation and an immediate evacuation is necessary."

A million questions ran through my head. But three got top billing:

What about the game?

What about my no-hitter?

Why do we have to leave right this second when the asbestos have probably been sitting around for years?

Because, really, whatever damage it was going to do to me was already done, right?

My awesome-amazing game was ruined.

Then, two days later, my entire season was ruined when the school held a parents' night. (At fancy, asbestos-free City Hall.)

The district had decided to funnel all the Luther kids to different schools until Luther was cleaned up. And because the public schools already had so many kids, some of us would get transferred to the private schools.

This already sounded awful.

And then today I got a packet in the mail from **PIPER BELL ACADEMY**.

UGH.

Piper Bell is a "progressive" school. My stepmom, Louie, said she thinks that means they have no "formal" grades. (Which maybe sounds cool but I have straight As for the first time ever! My grades *were* formal! They were wearing tuxedos and Piper Bell was going to make them wear sweatpants.)

AND all their sports are coed.

So far, I've been the only girl on Luther's baseball team, ever. And probably the only Golden Child.

But everyone knows Piper Bell has Devon DeWitt as a pitcher, and she's pretty good. We've never played each other, but I keep up with her stats in the local newspaper. (She hasn't been in a color photo, like me.)

They also have Mario Salamida, who hates me because he's never gotten a hit off me. In Little League. I've never actually played Piper Bell.

And I definitely don't want to play *for* Piper Bell.

Pretty much, I was being traded against my will.

And when that happens to a player—even the best, most Golden Child player ever—everything can go screwy.

It feels like a loss. I'm starting to think I'm going to kiss my win streak good-bye.

So that's why I started the playbook, Old Me.

To keep winning as much as possible.

I still can't believe they **TOOK AWAY MY UNICORN**.

Asbestos? More like as-**WORST**-os.

THE BEST UNIFORMS IN BASEBALL

- **Mo'Ne Davis's Mid-Atlantic Little League World Series Uniform**—The color combo is weird: blue and is it a dark purple or a bluish-brown? I don't know. But she wears it great, proving that when you have skills even a bruise-colored uniform is stylish.

- **The L.A. Dodgers**—They've used the same uniform model since they moved from Brooklyn to Los Angeles. Loyalty earns huge style points.

- **The Cardinals in the 1970s**—There's a color the sky turns where it doesn't even look real. They had uniforms that blue—the brightest in baseball history. I say, Why not?

- **The Chicago Cubs and New York Yankees**—The Cubs, lovable losers (until their unlikely World Series win after 108 years!!). The Yankees, dominant winners. Two teams who couldn't be more different but can both really wear pinstripes!

FIRST-DAY PLAY

Goal: Be the Golden Child of Piper Bell!

Action: I was the Golden Child at Luther Junior High because I was the baseball team's star. So step one is: let my reputation precede me. Step two? Wear my old Luther uniform just in case they don't know my reputation. **DUH.**

PROUD LION LOGO!

CONVERSATION PIECE! ♡

GOLD & BLACK COLORS WILL STAND OUT IN THE CROWD!

Post-Day Analysis:
April 15

Louie was dropping me off on her way to work—she does marketing or some other grown-up thing for a big soft drink company. Louie is great and probably knows everything, even if she doesn't act like someone who does.

"Do you really think you should wear your uniform?"

I checked it for stains but it was completely clean.

"Yeah, why not?"

"Just, you're going to a new school; maybe it's important to show school pride."

I wanted to ask how I could be proud when I didn't even know very much about Piper Bell yet, besides their sweatpants-wearing, non-formal grading system and the fact that since I got the letter I was going there, my hair started to do the weird shark-fin thing again. But I figured that Louie was entitled to her opinion.

Plus, I didn't want to get into the true reason for me wearing my uniform because then Louie would worry that I was nervous about all these changes, and worried parents are a bad ingredient if you're trying to keep a win streak. And I knew I had this under control. Or I hoped I did. The truth was, I wanted to play baseball. Even for Piper Bell. Baseball is who I am.

But I also wanted to keep my star status. I wanted the team to come to me, not the other way around. So by wearing my uniform, I would be announcing I was there without being all needy about it. It made perfect sense to me.

"There's time for that," I told Louie. "I just want them to know I already have a lot to be proud of."

"Hmm. Okay." Louie pressed the button for her favorite news station and kept driving.

UGH.

The "Hmm. Okay" is a kid kiss of death. It means that the grown-up in question thinks your idea is totally bad but they want you to figure out why.

"You think it's a bad idea?"

"Not necessarily."

Another grown-up mind trick!

WHAT 'NOT NECESSARILY' CAN MEAN
* GROWN-UP EDITION

SO WE'LL NEVER GET A PUPPY?

NOT NECESSARILY.

TRUE MEANING:

FORGET A PUPPY!

"Just . . . ," Louie said. "Make sure they know you're excited to be there as part of something new."

"But I'm not exactly," I sighed. "I was part of a good something old." And the Piper Bell team would get excited about that, to have a Luther Golden Child ready to play for them. I didn't say that, though.

"Just be humble."

"Okay," I told her. Just because I need to make my mark

doesn't mean I'm not humble! I'm the best humble person I know!

"And, remember, sometimes a smile and a hello are all you need."

Yes, if you're just a regular new kid, I thought. "My uniform will be a conversation piece. Don't worry. I've got this."

"Hmm. Okay. Well, at least you have a positive attitude."

NOOOOO!

She'd understand later when I gave her the update on how great my day was, I figured. I'd come home on the baseball team, totally adapted to my new environment. Another record for my record-setting year. I couldn't lose.

And I couldn't waste time deciphering grown-up mind games because . . .

WE WERE PULLING UP TO PIPER BELL. My strategy would be put into action!

It turned out that Piper Bell Academy was called an academy for a reason. Junior High was kid stuff compared to this place.

The driveway was made of fancy stones!

The trees looked like they had haircuts! Good haircuts!

There were bricks everywhere! (And not sad gray bricks like when your school has asbestos, but fancy red bricks that someone probably picked out of a catalog printed on heavy paper.

The kind of bricks that said, "You won't find asbestos here!")

And the students looked like they came out of a fancy cat-alog, too.

Some of them had on Piper Bell uniforms (jackets with gold buttons and pants—fancy ones) and some wore street clothes—actually, the choice was part of the whole "progres-sive" thing because Piper Bell was holding on to tradition **AND** embracing the new, said the brochure—but they really were like a private school playset that someone just opened that morning.

They were shiny and fresh-faced and I bet only drank water that had cut-up fruit floating in it. (I once went to get a haircut with Louie at her fancy salon where they had water with cut-up fruit in it, and Piper Bell reminds me of that.)

I did three quick in-and-out breaths and clapped my hands together, just like I did when I took the mound at the start of each inning.

"Wow, this place looks nice," Louie said. "You sure you don't want to wear the Piper Bell uniform for your first day? I have it in the trunk."

I waved her off like a bad sign from my coach. "Nah. This is the only uniform I need. It's totally me!"

I almost jumped out of the car before Louie had completely put the brakes on. I was one part excited, one part nervous, but the nervous part was **BIGGER**. I needed to imagine I was going off a high diving board: jumping right away was better than standing up there, staring down.

I did wish Diego were there (yeah, he was selected to go to Piper Bell, too, but of course wouldn't be because he was in Costa Rica). Since he was basically in the deepest part of the jungle, and his parents wanted him to be fully immersed in jungle life, we only got to talk sometimes, usually when he went into a nearby village and used a computer at an internet café to email or video-chat with me.

"Okay, see you later! Bye!"

With my backpack over my arm, I approached the front door of the school.

Over the door was a quote from Piper Bell: "Success and failure are equal, because in each we try."

Pfft.

Trying is fine, I guess.

But winning? That's the good stuff.

And really, school, you put a sign over your front door that says, "Hey, you might fail to learn anything! But you tried!"??

As I walked through the entrance, I listened to the announcer voices in my head that kind of follow my every move. (Not in a crazy way!)

Bob: One thing is clear as Garcia heads inside . . .

Judy: I can finish that sentence for you, Bob, and it's to say, she does NOT look like she fits in here. Her stepmom may have been right. Why would she wear something to make her stick out like a sore thumb?

≥INSIDE GABBY'S BRAIN≥

Bob and Judy were ticking me off.

Bob: Garcia's angry at our doubts, Judy. But I just don't know if this play is going to work.

SHUT IT, *Bob and Judy,* I thought.

But truth be told, I was getting some funny looks. Okay, *a lot* of funny looks.

WHAT I THOUGHT WOULD HAPPEN...

WHAT ACTUALLY HAPPENED.

VS

I was used to hecklers in the stands, though. It's how you know you're really good: you have a cheering section, but you also have opponents who live in fear of what you can do and sometimes make a point of saying so.

So I just strutted to my locker, the way I would strut back to the dugout even if I'd had a not-great inning. It was a mental thing.

THE STRUT THAT MAKES THE DIFFERENCE

Anyway, I didn't want to just fit in. I wanted to play baseball first, then fit in—but fit in in a winner kind of way. Diego sometimes says winning is too important to me, but it's not like that at all. It **IS** important to me, but the reasons aren't just so I can win and someone else can lose. I'd love if everyone could win. Winning is great! But they can't, so why wouldn't I want to be on the winning side? When I'm winning, I don't have as many questions about everything. When I win, I know I did the right thing. Not like now, writing this in my bedroom at the end of the day, wondering if I went wrong.

WHAT MAKES A WINNER/WHY I WANT TO WIN

- A winner knows what to do: the play to make, the right thing to say, exactly how to be.

- A winner is good to everyone, even the losing side. (This is important. Sore winning is as bad or worse than sore losing.)

- A winner gets picked for things, instead of trying to figure out how to ask for them.

- A winner doesn't have to worry, because winning means you don't doubt as much. **YOU'VE WON=YOU DID THINGS RIGHT.**

- A winner hardly ever wonders if things could have gone better, because they already went the best way they could!

When things were fuzzy, like at Piper Bell today—Had wearing my uniform been a mistake? Would the baseball team approach me?—I got this icky feeling in my stomach that I was playing everything all wrong. Maybe no one was talking to me because *they* were nervous. Maybe they didn't know about my high-dive strategy. Kids today have trouble making new friends, right? We were all wrapped up in our social media profiles and images and—ugh, that's just something I heard Louie say once.

Just jump, I tried to communicate to my new fellow students through a toothy smile, *I'm friendly!* Confident Golden Child strut or not, talking to me is as easy as the throw to first. Plus, everyone would want to know me once the baseball team recruited me. I was offering all these kids a head start on friendship with me.

But apparently my rep was getting in the way of making a good impression. Just not my *baseball* rep.

In homeroom, our teacher, Ms. Pluhar, had me stand at the front of the class to introduce myself.

So I said, "I'm Gabby Garcia. I used to go to Luther and they transferred me here."

Everyone started talking at once.

"Until they found a rat army in your school's basement, right?"

"Yeah, I heard that no one took the garbage out there for **YEARS**."

"I heard that sometimes rats fell into the lunch special and they cooked them and you ate them!"

"Wait, didn't all the Luther students have to get hazmat baths just to be decontaminated?"

"Those baths don't work."

"Eeew! She's a Luther Polluter!"

So I tried to reassure them there was nothing to worry about: "No, it was asbestos."

This doesn't help.

"As-what-sos?"

"Gross!"

"Luther Polluter!"

Ms. Pluhar finally settled the class down, but even she seemed to be keeping her distance from me. Really, a teacher!

By the time lunch period came, it was clear word got around because no one had talked to me all day. Not that I tried to talk to anyone either. Being called a Luther Polluter is kind of rough. And not the start to the baseball career I'd planned to have here.

I was definitely losing my strut, and then I overheard someone in my U.S. history class say, "I heard Gabby breathed on Katy Harris in their biology class and Katy went home with a fever."

I didn't know who Katy Harris was but I certainly didn't breathe on her. I had been practically holding my breath in since homeroom!

Strut **GONE**.

In the hallways, I ditched the toothy smile and started grinning to myself like I knew some great secret and would be willing to share it if someone would just talk to me. I even kind of tried to look like I was so into my interesting thoughts that I didn't *notice* the way no one was talking to me. And I crashed right into a janitor pushing a garbage can and fell down, taking the garbage can with me.

Fortunately, it was a recycling can, so when I was sprawled out on the floor, I was only covered with papers and a few plastic water bottles. But still, I looked even more like a Luther Polluter on my butt in the hall covered in discarded worksheets. The janitor started to pick up papers as other students swerved around us.

One student did reach out a hand. A boy in a plaid tie. And a pen behind his ear.

He helped me up as papers drifted off me to the floor. He saw the front of my jersey. "Luther, huh?" he said. "Wow, are you on the ball team there? I mean, were you? You've got a pitcher who's awesome."

I'M the awesome pitcher, I wanted to say, but I also thought I might cry. This day was nothing like I thought it would be. I wiped away the start of my tears. There's this saying, "There's no crying in baseball." My aim in life was to basically not cry, ever. It's another part of what makes a winner. So instead of answering, I mumbled "thank you" and zoomed away to my locker.

I didn't bother with my secret grin anymore.

I decided to skip lunch and go to the library, where I flipped through the spring training issue of *Sports Illustrated* I'd already read, hoping for an answer to leap from the pages. But everyone in the magazine had a team. I didn't. I had to regroup. There was no way the cafeteria crowd was going to make things better. If the whole student body thought I was covered with rat droppings or whatever, they didn't want to eat lunch with me.

I wouldn't want to eat lunch with a Luther Polluter, either. Or probably play baseball with one.

So what I feared has already happened.

It's hard to write this, but my win streak is **OFFICIALLY OVER**. I have to chalk up today as a **LOSS**.

WINS: 0
LOSSES: 1

REASONS WHY IT STINKS DIEGO IS IN COSTA RICA

- We usually watch spring training baseball games together and this year we couldn't because no one in Costa Rica cares about spring training.

- He missed my unicorn. And my partial unicorn.

- If I need an uplifting sports highlight or fact to get me through the day, I now have to send him an email that he might not get for hours, instead of just slapping his arm and saying, "Hey, I need some sports trivia." This is very inconvenient.

- If anyone would be excited about transferring to a whole new school, it's Diego. He can go anywhere and make new friends instantly.

TAKING A MULLIGAN

Goal: To wash the stench of Luther Polluter off my person, get my new classmates to appreciate my greatness, and take my rightful spot on the baseball team.

Action: Mulligans are technically a golf thing. Golf is **SOOOOOO** boring. I mostly don't know much about it. But the one thing it has that's pretty neat is called a "mulligan." It's really just a do-over but it's probably named after some lousy golfer named Mulligan who needed to do things over a lot. So today is meant to be a do-over of yesterday, and instead of my uniform, I will have baked goods to **WIN PEOPLE OVER**.

Post-Day Analysis:
April 16

A quick replay of yesterday for perspective . . .

My first day at Piper Bell was awful and stinky because, well, everyone thought I was awful and stinky. And losses happen.

But I **HATE** losses. Every one puts you further and further into a losing streak. The opposite of a winning streak. I can't get my life back to **PERFECT** if I keep having setbacks.

Dad picked me up from Piper Bell, and he must have been able to tell something was wrong because he asked the question I was dreading: "How was school?"

How could he have been so inconsiderate? Couldn't he see that school was **NOT GOOD**?

It was like a press conference when they ask the losing team how they think they played. But they lost! Who wants to talk about that???

So instead of answering honestly, I gave the answer adults dread: "Fine."

It was partly because I was in a bad mood and partly because my little brother, Peter, was in the car and I definitely didn't want to give him anything to use against me.

"That good, huh?" Dad can always tell when I am "stewing" about something (a phrase he **LOVES** as much as actual stew). Unfortunately, he didn't know not to bring it up.

I sank into the car seat, wanting to get home and regroup for the next day.

Peter laughed: "I bet Gabby has no friends!"

"I do too. Or, I will. Once Diego gets back."

Of course, Diego wasn't going to be back forever (well, a little more than a month) and had been the one other Luther student picked to go to Piper Bell, which would have been really good luck if Diego wasn't also in Costa Rica with monkeys and coconuts and whatever else they have there. "Or, maybe even tomorrow."

I was trying to tell myself that for sure tomorrow (which is now today) **HAD** to be the day the baseball team would make sure I was on it. They probably just didn't do that sort of stuff on a Monday.

"Whatever. The only way you can get friends is if you bribe everyone."

I was trying to come up with a nasty comment to make in return, but then I replayed Peter's words: **BRIBE EVERYONE**.

"Peter, I will never say this again so pay attention: you are brilliant!"

Then I turned to my dad.

"Dad, how do you feel about a little baking?"

And this morning, I walked into Piper Bell a changed woman. I had a lunch bag brimming with Dad's Monster Cookies—they had oatmeal, chocolate chips, and M&Ms, so that's why they were called monsters.

And though I hadn't quite made peace with wearing the Piper Bell uniform, I **WAS** wearing school colors, red and black, in the form of my dad's vintage Michael Jordan Bulls jersey with red high-tops and black jeans. Jordan is my dad's favorite player.

I could barely pay attention in my other classes because I was so excited for lunch. This would be my mulligan moment, and my win streak would barely be tarnished. I didn't even get upset when a fashionista-type asked with a frown, "What is **JORDAN**?"

So when lunch finally did roll around, I made a beeline for Devon DeWitt's table. I knew what she looked like because I'd seen her pitch in the tournament games they air on community cable, and I recognized her from a photo in the community paper. (Not color, like mine.) They only put your picture in if you're pretty good, so she's competition in a way, but I figured we'd speak the same language. And, if she cared about her team at all, she'd want me on it.

I plopped down without waiting for an invitation because I had cookies to share. Plus, the only way to recover from a loss is to **BRING IT** all to your next game. And bringing cookies wasn't the same as having to ask to be on the team, which could be awkward and also make it seem too much like I needed the team more than it needed me. Cookies were a gesture that said, "Sure, I'd be open to an offer to be on the team"—and a winning gesture at that.

For a long second—or maybe several seconds—Devon blinked at me. In slow motion. It was weird.

(Blink)

(Blink)

(Blink)

"I saw you pitch once against Franklin Middle. You're good," she finally said to me.

"Yeah, I saw you against the Judson Junior High team. So are you."

Since we've never played against each other, it was a big deal to admit that we've seen each other and even bigger to give compliments.

She blinked again and went back to talking to a boy I recognized as Ryder Mills, who's a pretty decent catcher.

But it wasn't like she told me to go away. I felt on the verge of my first mini-win.

Until Mario Salamida butt-flopped into the seat next to me. (Like a belly flop but your butt hits the chair as hard as your belly would hit water.)

"What is *she* doing here?" he asked Devon. About me.

Mario **JUST. CAN'T. DEAL.** Since our Little League days,

he never has once gotten a hit off me, so I've always let it slide. (But not him. He never gets to slide when he goes against me because he can't get on base! Ha!)

"I don't know, she sat here," Devon said. "This isn't some movie where I have to be mean because she's new."

Mario's nostrils flared up but he didn't say anything. I liked that Devon could tell him off.

I hoped she'd like my bribes. Um, cookies.

I got to talk to Diego last night—on the phone and everything. (His parents want him to really understand deep-jungle living, so he's pretty "entrenched" when it comes to regular communicating.) He didn't understand why I didn't just talk to the coach, or the team. "It's not a weakness to just say what you want sometimes."

"But I need them to be **EXCITED** to have me. If I'm Mike Trout, I don't go to the Yankees and say, 'Please put me on the team.' It's better mojo if you know you're wanted."

(Old Me, Mike Trout is a really, really good Major League Baseball center fielder for the Los Angeles Angels, and I am sure he'd agree with me.)

"But you're not Mike Trout and it's junior high, not the major leagues," Diego told me. I wished the phone would get crackly so I didn't have to hear all this.

"Well, on a junior high level, I'm Mike Trout–caliber, so it's the same to me. It's a win streak thing."

"Okay, I'm not going to argue with you. I get enough flak from the monkeys," Diego said, and then told me how a spider monkey took a banana right out of his hand as he was eating breakfast that morning. It was a very Diego thing to have happen.

So, even though Diego didn't quite get it, I had my cookies and I had hope when I walked into the cafeteria.

Bob: It's a beautiful day for making things happen, isn't it, Judy?

Judy: Well, Bob, I agree. This should be a day when nothing goes wrong. Gabby's got cookies to share. If she's not on the team with everyone at this table as a future BFF by the end of the period, well, I'll be very confused.

Bob: Yes, she and Devon should hit it off no matter what.

Judy: Mario Salamida is a factor.

Bob: Eh, who's worried about him? If Gabby can get the rest of the team, that's all she needs to take her spot on the roster and get back to winning.

Judy: Let's go to the table, see how these cookies are working.

So it was me, Devon, Mario, Ryder, and a few other kids who I guessed were on the baseball team. Devon was complaining about a pop quiz in her English class, and most of them were chewing and nodding sympathetically.

"Seriously, guys, pop quizzes should be outlawed," she said. Everyone agreed and then I just plunged in.

"Pop quizzes are *the worst*," I said. "But you know what isn't? These cookies I brought. My dad made a bunch and they're really good."

It was crazy how fast everyone stopped talking and turned toward me when I said "cookies." But to growing kids, cookies are essential.

"Sweet," Ryder said. "My mom's been baking with kale, so I could use some sugar."

"I wish anyone at my house baked," Devon said, using chopsticks to lift a piece of sushi from her bento box. "It's takeout central for us."

And now they were eagerly waiting for me to produce the cookies.

But there was a problem.

Also in my lunch was a wrap. A wrap that was filled, it looked like, with the French beef stew my dad made for dinner last night. No one ate it because stew should not be eaten when you live in Georgia and it's April and 80 degrees outside. Well, my dad ate it. (See—he **LOVES** stew!)

More importantly, stew shouldn't be in a lunch bag with cookies.

It was really **WITH** the cookies, too, as in just everywhere inside the bag.

It didn't look good. If possible, it looked worse than when we didn't eat it for dinner the first time.

It looked like maybe an animal had used my lunch bag as a toilet.

Bob: *Oh no, this looks ugly.*

Bob was really right. I was about to say I'd forgotten the cookies when Mario actually pulled my lunch sack away from me and snapped, "Well, are there cookies or not?"

I pulled back and the lunch sack launched into the air. Cookies and goo went everywhere. Mostly goo. Goo travels faster, I guess.

And it was **EVERYWHERE**.

Stew goo splattered the lunch table and a corner of Ryder's algebra book and the napkin dispenser.

Judy: *Bob, I can't look.*
Bob: *Oh, you're right, Judy.*

But Bob and Judy were just imaginary voices in my head. With my very
real eyes, I could see the goo land on
Mario.

Splat!

"What the . . . ." Mario looked
down at his stew-goo-covered
shirt and his face turned green.

Bob: *Mario's getting up. He's running to the garbage can.*

Judy: *His face is halfway in the garbage can. Yes! Mario Salamida
just hurled!*

Bob: *The entire cafeteria had to have heard that retching.*

Everyone was watching Mario. At least they weren't looking at my gross lunch.

Then Mario looked up and glared at me, like I was the bad
guy on one of the courtroom shows Louie watches. "This isn't
over, *Gaggy Garcia!*"

I didn't know anything had even started.

Devon looked at Mario and then looked at me and then
looked at the goo-covered cookies.

"I think I'll pass."

My appetite was totally gone because I could definitely

chalk up the day as another loss. One more and my winning streak would officially be a losing streak.

WINS: 0
LOSSES: 2 (plus stew)

INSPIRING THINGS ATHLETES HAVE SAID
ABOUT LOSING

- "Show me a good loser, and I'll show you a loser."
  —Vince Lombardi

- "I hate to lose more than I like to win." —Larry Bird

- "Nobody remembers who finished second but the guy who finished second." —Bobby Unser

- "I could never stand losing. Second place didn't interest me. I had a fire in my belly." —Ty Cobb

- "You wouldn't have won if we'd beaten you."
  —Yogi Berra

THE SCOPE, DITCH, AND SWITCH

Goal: Undo some of the damage of the day before by bringing a normal (not-Gaggy) lunch.

Action: It's as simple as it sounds: 1. I scope my lunch. 2. If it's gross, I ditch my lunch. 3. Then I switch the ditched lunch for something normal.

Post-Day Analysis:
April 17

The day of the goo had been another day of answering my dad's inquiries about school with "fine." Because nothing had been fine about it. Everyone at Piper Bell had seen or heard about the stew goo, and the worst part was, I felt as if the baseball team—the exact people I wanted to impress—were the ones who probably disliked me the most.

So no one said that, but it's not like I stuck around to take a survey of what they thought of me.

I had to regroup. Again. Regrouping alone was hard. I probably wouldn't hear from Diego for at least a few days, and I really didn't have anyone else I wanted to share my colossal failures with.

So, okay, I know I **COULD** have mentioned the bad lunch thing to my dad, but after all the help he gave me with the cookies, I didn't want to. When I have a few bad games, my usual way to deal is not to dwell on defeat. I usually think positive and figure out my next moves. Besides, it was all so busy around our house with Louie working on a big project and Peter being annoying. I liked to be the low-maintenance kid with the big talent.

Also, my dad loves to cook. The problem was, the things he makes might be fine to eat at home, but not so much as leftovers in my lunch. Luther had a cafeteria (oh, what I would give for those extra french fries now)—but Piper Bell has students bring their lunches "to ensure adherence to our families' preferred dietary needs." (From the handbook, and I think it just means that because Piper Bell is fancier and progressive, a cafeteria here couldn't just serve pizza sticks and call it a day. At Luther, we called it Pizza Stick Wednesday. Some of the kids at Piper Bell had personal pizzas made by their at-home chefs—not smushed leftovers from their dads—or sandwiches on bread with lots of healthy seeds. No pizza sticks in sight.)

So I had the Scope, Ditch, and Switch. But, yes, I went to bed hoping some kind of daughter-father ESP might allow me to transmit a message to Dad in his sleep: a message that said, *Do not pack last night's ceviche in my lunch.*

Ceviche is delicious: it's a refreshing fish salad with lime and cilantro, and my dad's ceviche is way better than his stew. But day-old ceviche in my lunch would be **NOT REALLY GOOD**. Fish has a way of telling people it's there, and the stew kind of already did that.

So this morning, I scoped my lunch and saw ceviche was exactly what Dad had packed me.

It was time to ditch the fish.

The ditch part of my plan was maybe the most complicated. To do it, I needed to rely on timing and wits and our next-door neighbors' dog, Dumpster.

Dumpster is a hyperactive mutt with a bucket-shaped body and the energy of several puppies.

Also, Dumpster eats **ANYTHING**.

Most dogs will eat anything, but if Dumpster could, he'd hop the fence and learn to use a fork and knife and sit down to dinner at our house, after eating dinner with Mr. and Mrs. Dumpster next door. (Not their real name.) Dumpster would eat a meal at every house in our cul-de-sac and take home doggy bags if he could. (But he wouldn't have anything left to put in the bags.)

So, with Louie already at work early prepping her team for a huge upcoming board meeting, and my dad in the shower, and Peter busy thinking Peter thoughts about how to be irritating in new and different ways, I ran the play:

First, I ran outside with the thermos of ceviche, hoping to hear Dumpster.

I couldn't just dump fish in the neighbors' yard.

No noise.

Maybe the dog was inside.

Then, like magic, I heard Dumpster barking.

He could smell the food.

Or maybe Dumpster and I had ESP.

I ran to the hole in the fence. It was the exact right size for getting rid of an unwanted lunch. Dumpster's nose was already sticking through. I scooped out the ceviche and tried not to hurl as I heard the dog slurping it up.

Then I dashed back inside and raided the fridge for regular stuff to make a regular sandwich. There's plenty of regular stuff because Peter is a "picky eater," which just means he demands a different, annoying food no matter what we're eating.

I was trying to unscrew the cap from the mayo when my dad shouted from upstairs.

"Gabby, have you seen my phone?"

"Oh yeah . . . Dad was shouting for you, Gabby," Peter said without looking up.

Oh no. "What did you tell him?"

"I thought you were in the bathroom."

"Gabby, you out of the bathroom?? Can you see if my phone is down there?"

My hands got sweaty.

"Why didn't he ask you to look for the phone?" I muttered to Peter as I struggled with the mayo.

"He did; I didn't see it." Peter pointed to the mayo. "What are you doing?"

"It's . . . for my hair." I saw that on TV once.

"That stick-uppy thing? Good luck, Freako." Peter shook his head.

Still trying to take the cap off the mayo, I peered around frantically for my dad's phone. I couldn't open the mayo.

"Never mind, I'll come down."

"No!" I yelled, slapping turkey onto bread as I heard my dad's footsteps. I threw the mayo back in the fridge and slammed it shut. I spun and crammed the sandwich into my lunch sack. Dad came into the kitchen, where I leaned against the counter, my body blocking the bag as if Dad could see through things.

"And what is this?" Dad said as he reached behind my back.

I almost wet my pants.

He held up his phone and looked at Peter and me. "Oh, kids, your powers of detection are weak."

I breathed again.

Close one.

But I made it.

The Scope, Ditch, and Switch was a success!

WINS: 1 (because I didn't get caught!)
LOSSES: 2

MAJOR LEAGUE BALLPARK FOODS THAT NEED TO GET IN MY BELLY

• **Dodger Dog** at Dodgers Stadium (Los Angeles Dodgers)—It's simple but a classic.

• **Victory Knot Pretzel** at Guaranteed Rate Field (Chicago White Sox)—You know what's better than a normal-sized hot pretzel from the mall that you eat on a bench somewhere while watching people shop? A pretzel bigger than your whole face that you eat while watching a baseball game!

- **Nachos on a Stick** at Miller Park (Milwaukee Brewers)—Diego says I'll eat any food if you put it on a stick. I say, why wouldn't I?

- **Carne Asada Fries** at Petco Park (San Diego Padres)—My dad had these once and has not stopped talking about them. So I need to try them.

- **Fried Green Tomatoes** at SunTrust Park (Atlanta Braves)—My home team, and a perfect Atlanta food.

- **Ice Cream Sundaes** served in tiny helmets (all ballparks, that I know of)—Ice cream is already great but you put it in a mini baseball helmet and it's even better. Someday, I will have a helmet from every field.

Post-Day Analysis:
April 18, afternoon recap

Sigh. Sigh. Sigh. And not just little "oh well" sighs. Sighs of **DEEP FAILURE**. Sighs of agony. Sighs of someone who **JUST. CAN'T. WIN.** I'm writing this in the bathroom just so no one bothers me. No one writes in the bathroom if things are going right.

Two days of new, normal lunches do not seem to matter. So, fine, I've avoided bringing anything gross and weird, but no one was exactly running up to me and saying, "Wow, what a great sandwich you have! Be our friend. Come to the baseball team, we know how great you are!"

And let's face it, in order for my **BEST YEAR EVER** to remain intact I can't be **FRIENDLESS**. Or **BASEBALL TEAM-LESS**. Especially that one.

So even though the Scope, Ditch, and Switch was technically a successful play and one I'll keep doing to maintain a normal lunch, I have to take away the win I gave myself. Because it hasn't paid off at school.

It seems like my time limit for making an impression is running out after only three days. No one cares that much about a new kid, and three days in, they're kind of over me. Even the Luther Polluter stuff has died down.

I'm just sort of **THERE**.

OTHER THINGS THAT ARE JUST THERE

- Oatmeal without cinnamon

- The color beige

- The jigsaw puzzle Peter and I started two years ago that remains unfinished in our basement (it's of a kind of brown landscape that makes me yawn when I look the box, so why finish?)

- Goldfish, the most frequently overlooked pet

It's like I don't exist. Or just half exist. I'm Piper Bell's goldfish. They'll feed me enough so I don't die but they're not going to take me out to play with.

Apologies to all the goldfish out there, but half existing is sort of like losing.

I didn't really think about how to be the new kid beyond instantly being a baseball star, just like I was at Luther.

And the baseball team hasn't asked me to join. I even wandered by the field after school yesterday, probably hoping that, by ESP, they'd look up and see me and say, "Oh my gosh! How are you not on the team yet?"

But that didn't happen. They didn't even see me. I really have zero ESP skills.

Besides breaking my win streak, racking up all these losses is making it hard to know how to get my win. I just want to play baseball and have friends and not feel like a goldfish. Is that too much to ask?

Could I scope, ditch, and switch my whole existence?

Someone's knocking.

Louie . . .

Okay, so I'm writing this in my room, at my desk, not in the bathroom. I feel a little better. Louie wanted to make sure I was feeling okay—I was in the bathroom a long time, I guess—and I told her in the most parent-worry-free way possible that I was kind of sort of hoping that by now the baseball team would have recruited me.

And she said that a lot of times, people don't know what we want because they're so caught up in their own thoughts and wishes and wants. And then she said, if there's not a way to come right out and say what you want, is there a way to show it?

And there just happens to be one.

WINS: 0
LOSSES: 3 (but on the verge of correction!)

THE HOME RUN

Goal: Remind the baseball team they have a star in their midst.

Action: If you can't **TELL** them how great you are, you must **SHOW** them. Even though I strongly believe the team should have approached **ME**, I'm giving them the benefit of the doubt. So, while I don't want to **ASK** to be on the team, I **DO** want to demonstrate to them what they're missing. In a big way! Today, I'm going to have a movie moment.

Post-Day Analysis:
April 22

Okay, fine, I thought coming to Piper Bell was going to be different. I mean, usually when a superstar gets traded to a new team, that team is really excited to have them. That

...as what I expected. Instant recognition. I'd been on a win streak after all.

But, hey, it was probably the media.

I had what's called a perception problem.

Being a new kid when the school year was almost over probably wasn't helping—the team's season was well under way (and they had zero losses, so it wasn't like they were desperate for help). And then, I'd had the uniform thing, the stew goo, the Luther Polluter rep. What's more, the Penguins had a full roster. **AND** maybe they were intimidated by **ME**. What if I said no, I didn't want to be on their team, because I had a team? These were all possibilities.

Or maybe no one cared. But I was going to make sure they did.

I gave myself the weekend to recharge. I watched a lot of baseball with my dad. It was the right move, because I saw teams that had looked horrible in spring training starting to win. A lot of times, it turns out, pre-season doesn't matter once the real stuff starts.

So I decided to look at my first week at Piper Bell as a sort of "pre-season." I didn't have to play my best because it didn't count. I'd just been testing stuff out. I knew that wasn't exactly true, but I told myself it was.

This week, I had to make it count. For that, I couldn't count on anyone but myself. No uniform, no cookies, just me.

And when I told Diego my movie-moment plan during a choppy, noisy Skype session—He wasn't kidding about the monkeys! They are loud!—he said he wished he could see it in action. Diego wouldn't say that if he didn't mean it.

So, after school, I headed over to the field where the team practiced and took a seat on the bleachers, just past the first-base dugout. This boy Johnny Madden sat a few rows up from me. I waved at him as he gave me a quizzical look. He was in my algebra class and he was also the student who'd helped me up that first day when I'd landed in the spilled recycling. He must have been the team stats-keeper because he had a big logbook opened on his lap.

JOHNNY MADDEN

JOHNNY MADDEN

(a.k.a. OLYMPIC LEVEL MATHLETE)

Height: Definitely taller than me
Build: Suitable for tie wearing and clipboard carrying, apparently
Sport: Olympic-level mathlete
Favorite Athlete: To be determined during extensive conversation
Quote: "Imagination is more important than knowledge."
—Albert Einstein

Practice was already going. The coach, whose name is Coach Hollylighter, had the players on the field and she was hitting balls as other players ran the bases. The team practiced throwing to one another to try to get players out.

It wasn't a hard drill but it showed they were pretty good as a team. The ball landed with solid *thwacks* as each player threw it to the next. I almost got carried away by the rhythm. **THWACK! THWACK! THWACK!** I could listen to that sound all day.

Fortunately, Coach Hollylighter handed the bat to one of the players—ugh, Mario—and had him step up to bat. Devon was on the mound.

I'd been waiting for the batting portion of practice.

I called my catlike reflexes into action, scooting my butt to the very edge of the bleachers. I had the sense this was my moment. My winning-season winning life was about to restart **NOW**.

Mario looked over and gave me a weird eyeballing. Maybe I'd be wondering what I was doing there, too. Plus, there's that whole he's-never-gotten-a-hit-off-me thing, so my presence probably bothered him.

Devon went into her windup and lobbed a fastball. Mario took a big swing and missed.

I started to wonder if he couldn't hit *her* pitches, either.

She threw again. Another strike. Wow, she was better than I remembered.

But Mario got a piece of the next pitch, and the hit was exactly what I was hoping for. A high pop fly headed to center field. I pulled on my mitt and leapt from the bleachers. I didn't look anywhere but at the ball. I had their attention, I knew it.

I ignored Mario's voice shouting, "Gaggy, get off the field!"

I ignored the other exclamations of "What is she doing?" "Is that the Luther Polluter?" "We're practicing here!"

They'd be practicing their expressions of wonder and awe soon enough. That pop fly was my calling card.

Glove outstretched, I made one beautiful, ballet-like leap into center field, trying to cover as much ground as I could. The ball was coming down, headed for my glove. I was going to have it.

The ball and a **WIN**.

THWACK!

The ball hit my mitt and my hand closed around it.

SMASH.

UH-OH.

Was that blood?

"OUCH! WHAT ARE YOU DOING? OUCH!!! MY NOSE!"

The center fielder, this girl Madeleine who was in my chemistry class, was looking at me with a blood-smeared face. She held her nose as blood oozed out of it. I touched my own nose, which was fine.

"I'm sorry! I'm sorry! Are you okay?" My voice was **VERY SCREECHY**.

"NO!" she yelled, and I looked away from all the blood.

I might be good at sports but I am not good at blood.

I didn't want to hurt anyone! But Madeleine seemed more bloody and angry than actually hurt. And the ball was in my glove.

Still, my movie moment turned from inspiring sports movie to terrifying horror movie.

So I stopped myself from holding the ball in the air and saying, "I got it!"

"What were you thinking?" The voice was an adult voice. An authority voice. A coach voice.

I turned and was looking up at Coach Hollylighter. She's very tall with the kind of stick-straight hair that probably never does a shark-fin thing. She has freckles but even though freckles usually make me think someone will be easy to talk to (I don't know why, I just do), her freckles are intimidating. Maybe because at that moment, they framed the very permanent-seeming frown on her face.

She probably has a kind and supportive face when it's not quite so angry.

But it was **SUPER**-angry.

"Um, hi, I'm Gabby Garcia," I said. Because I didn't really know what I was thinking but I thought if I tried to explain the movie-moment thing, Coach Hollylighter was not going to like it.

"I know who you are."

I was pretty excited when she said that. I figured she did—I knew all the top Piper Bell players' names—and this confirmed it. But then she continued.

"I know who you are, Gabby Garcia. But my question is, what are you doing?"

"Um, introducing myself?"

"You thought you'd introduce yourself by almost giving one of your classmates a concussion???"

I looked at Madeleine, who had an ice pack against her nose. She was surrounded by members of the team who were not looking as impressed with me as I thought they'd be. But she definitely didn't have a concussion.

"That wasn't the point," I said. I thought about telling her how I was going for a big movie moment and how it was *supposed* to play out. **LIKE THIS**:

The ball is in the air. It practically calls my name: "Gabby, bet you can't catch me!"

I leap from the bleachers, eagle eyes on the ball dropping from the sky.

Every member of the team—even Mario, who should be running to first—stops what they're doing to watch.

"It's Gabby Garcia, from Luther . . . ," someone would say in a hushed tone.

They know magic is about to be made.

The ball floats down from the heavens. I gracefully stretch out my arm, pirouetting toward the ball and my future. It's a magical dance and, at last, the ball lands beautifully in my glove. The team applauds and lifts me onto their shoulders because they all know they have found the missing piece in their best season ever!

Then, perhaps, confetti.

But the eyeballs on me were not like that at all.

And there was definitely no confetti.

So I remembered something my dad once said: "A wise man once said nothing."

Instead of explaining, I just said, "I'm sorry."

I did mean that. Because Madeleine's nose had to hurt and it was my fault.

Coach Hollylighter sighed. One of those grown-up, why-do-I-have-to-do-this sighs for people who are just too tired to form words. (Which is most grown-ups I've met.)

"Look, I know you can play, but it is late in the season and taking on a new player could disrupt things when they're going well. You can try out tomorrow, though. Without any displays like that."

The Penguins were undefeated, so I guessed that was what she meant. But wouldn't I help make them **MORE** undefeated? I was a little surprised she didn't say, "Hey, that was violent and scary but you really can catch and, let's face it, we all know who you are, Gabby Garcia, so will you join our team, please?"

We could have avoided Madeleine's bloody nose if she'd just approached me like that right away. But I got the impression that Coach Hollylighter probably was someone who liked things kept a certain way, and that meant not adding to an already-full roster with a **DISRUPTION**.

So getting a tryout was something. And I hadn't had to actually **ASK** for it.

"A tryout sounds great!" I lied. "I won't let you down."

Coach Hollylighter raised one of her eyebrows.

"Well, let's just see if you can avoid plowing into someone and we'll go from there."

All in all, I decided to call this day a **WIN** (despite putting Madeleine on the disabled list—**ACCIDENTALLY!**). A tryout is still a chance and a chance is all I need.

WINS: 1
LOSSES: 3

THE GREATS: MO'NE DAVIS
Little League Pitcher for the Taney Dragons

Age: 15
From: Philadelphia, Pennsylvania
Known for: Being one of two girls to play in the 2014 Little League World Series
Why she's great: First girl to win and pitch a shutout in the series' sixty-eight-year history! Yeah, throwing like a girl.

MO'NE DAVIS

(a.k.a. MY BIGGEST
INSPIRATION)

(Who even thought of saying that as an insult when it's **OBVIOUSLY** a compliment!)

Odd fact: Despite amazing baseball skills, considers **BASKETBALL** her first sport

TAKE IT TO THE LIMIT

Goal: After my last play went pretty *foul* (**HA!** I kill me sometimes), I need to show leadership and skill beyond a normal seventh-grade player.

Action: I would make up for my movie moment by showing them everything I know about baseball. Everyone likes an expert, right?

Post-Day Analysis:
April 23

Okay, so I really needed the tryout to go perfectly. Did it? Well, hmm, maybe writing about it here, in the calming confines of my room, will help me decide.

I might have been calling it a win, but in the back of my head, I was worried that yesterday's show for Coach

Hollylighter and the team was more of a loss. Overall, my Piper Bell losing streak was a lot like trailing toilet paper from the bottom of your shoe—I just wanted to get it off me but I didn't want to touch it directly, and even when I did think it was gone, I was worried I'd look down and find out I was still dragging it around.

Like today, I showed up for biology and realized I forgot to finish my paper on photosynthesis. And in algebra, I almost turned in my homework without realizing I didn't finish the last three problems. Johnny Madden caught it when I passed my paper forward.

He turned around. "You forgot to do the last three," he said. "They're simple, though. You can probably knock them out in no time and just turn in your paper at the end of class."

I liked that he had faith I could just take care of them so quickly, instead of being one of those boys who assume you must need help because it's math. I'm good at math. A lot of girls are good at math, thank you very much. (Just like we're good at throwing.)

Also, I noticed his eyes were the same color as a ball field. He was kind of odd. He wore a tie every day and toted around extra math books that weren't for class and sometimes forgot to even leave the classroom because he was doing extra equations in a notebook, I think for fun. He was cute. I got the sense that people didn't notice this about him.

But I did. I had yesterday, in the bleachers, before I knocked Madeleine out.

"And don't worry about your tryout," he said at the end of the period. "Just don't be afraid to show them what made you such a good pitcher at Luther."

"How did you know I pitched at Luther?"

"We've all heard of Gabby Garcia," he said. "I just didn't recognize you on the first day. But when you showed up in my algebra class, I told Coach to recruit you. She's a stickler. She told me we have our lineup, and if you wanted to play, you'd say something. So I was really glad you showed up yesterday."

At least someone had been. But before I could answer, he walked out of class. Holy schmoley! He'd **TOLD** Coach Hollylighter to recruit me! That was really nice! But why hadn't he told me what she'd said before?

WAYS JOHNNY MADDEN IS STRANGE

• Wears a tie

• Great at math and doesn't make a big deal about it

• Seems to love math so much he has extra textbooks about it

66

- In fact, what is he doing in regular algebra anyway?

- They probably don't have a class smart enough for him.

- Totally went to bat for me (**HA!**) with Coach Hollylighter

- Just gets around to telling me **NOW**

- And then, walks away!

- Walks away!! Gah!

It gave me a boost of confidence, that was for sure. And it gave me an idea.

Who I was had nothing to do with my uniform or about big movie moments. I was Gabby Garcia, practically an expert at any sport. But especially baseball.

I needed to make that clear at my tryout today.

So, fine, the Penguins were good, but what if there was a reason I was here, and they needed me? Maybe all of this asbestos stuff was some twisted way to bring me here, to be a game-changer for the Penguins. I'm not into horoscopes or all that weird fortune-telling stuff, but I **AM** superstitious, like any respectable athlete. And like any respectable athlete, sometimes I get a feeling about things.

And I'd talked myself into it: they needed me. That was my feeling.

So I got to practice right on time.

When I saw Coach Hollylighter, I gave her my best "I promise not to wound anyone" smile. Then I said, "I'm here for practice."

She held up a finger. "I need to remind you that this is a tryout. We're a strong team and we need to make sure you're a good fit. I'm not actively seeking new players, even great ones."

I nodded. Darn, she really was a stickler. I'd been hoping she'd just go with the practice thing and I'd be on the team. But, okay, maybe Coach Hollylighter was just tricking me a little about the tryout. She was calling it a tryout, but really I was just joining in a practice and as I practiced I would also be trying out. She

HAD called me a great player, after all.

I was back in business. I was going to entirely shed this losing streak like it never existed.

"What should I do?" I asked Coach Hollylighter.

"Well, we're doing our Round of Catch warm-up. How about you take shortstop for that drill? It's how we start practice."

Catch was how we ended practice at Luther. But, okay, I could deal with that. However, I'm a pitcher. Not a shortstop.

"I'm a pitcher. Shouldn't I be there?"

Coach didn't answer right away. I tried to make eye contact with Johnny, who had a calculator and was entering player stats into a big logbook, but he didn't look up. After what he'd said in algebra, I'd been hoping for some support on his end. But I guessed he felt about math the way I did about baseball: when he was doing it, that was all he could think about.

"DeWitt, you okay stepping off the mound for a bit? For Gabby's tryout."

Devon did her slow-blink thing. She did not seem okay with it.

But she tossed the ball to Ryder Mills and stepped off the mound. "Yeah, whatever," she said, and walked past me without any eye contact. She would be grateful for me soon enough, though!

I didn't get to notice it so much last week, because I was so busy smashing into Madeleine, but the grass on the field is cushier than the grass at Luther, and the dirt isn't as dusty. It was as tidy a field as the rest of Piper Bell, like it should have been covered in plastic like my grandma's furniture so that my dirty cleats couldn't mess it up.

But even though it was different from Luther's scrappy field, it was a ball field. Ahhhhh. With each step, I felt stronger, like one of those nature specials where the baby animals take their first steps and then suddenly are able to run. I was becoming **ME** again. Yup, baseball is my game, and even more than that, baseball is **ME**.

On the mound, I could see everything. Maybe that's why I've always liked being a pitcher. When you're right at the center of everything, you know exactly what to do. You're already winning, in a way.

It made playing good baseball a lot clearer than a lot of other stuff in life.

Ryder tossed me the ball and I knew to throw it to Mario.

"Heads up, Salamida," I called.

He said, "Duh, Gaggy," but caught it and threw to Devon at shortstop.

We circled around like that and I could feel Coach Hollylighter watching me, so I tried to dazzle her a little by giving tips to the team.

"Devon, you're twisting your wrist on the catch too much! But good throw!"

"Mario, you're way off the bag. Stay close."

"Ryder? You looked away from the ball! Heads up! You're a catcher! How will you frame a pitch if you're not watching it? Be José Molina!"

I tried to give a tip to every player whose name I knew. Except Madeleine. I just said "Good job!" to her. She seemed sensitive, plus I did almost break her nose. But when I looked over at Coach Hollylighter, I couldn't tell what she was thinking.

"Let's take some batting practice," she said. "Gabby, do you mind pitching to the team?"

"Not at all!" Of course I wanted to pitch. It's what I **DO**.

Right away, I noticed that Dinah Labuto, the first batter, needed some bat alignment help. "Hey, you're turning your foot."

"I always turn my foot."

"Yeah, she's good that way," Devon said from the on-deck circle.

"But what if she's better with it the other way? Mookie Wilson turned his foot and then he straightened it out and his average went up ten points!" This is true, and if Diego had been there, he would have backed me up. He wasn't, and when I looked at Johnny, hoping his statistical wizardry would mean he knew the same fact, he just gave me a thumbs-up, which was nice but not very helpful.

Dinah didn't straighten her foot. And she didn't get a hit off me in ten pitches, which I thought proved my point.

Before Devon stepped up, I tossed a practice throw to my current catcher, a girl named Elizabeth Wu, who was in for Ryder as he waited for his at bat. She almost toppled over as she reached up for the ball.

"I think your glove needs to be a little higher," I told her. "Trust me. Remember, you're not just catching. You're framing and blocking."

I was using my pitching lingo with expertise and authority.

Elizabeth listened and raised her glove. On my next practice pitch, she easily grabbed it out of the air. "See, you got it! Just follow through on your throw to the mound."

Mario, who was manning first base for the drill, let out a massive groan. "Gaggy is bossy today, huh?"

"Hey." I turned to him. "Are you paying attention out there?"

I thought I was doing pretty good, showing my skills and knowledge of the game so far. I was being a helpful guide to the players who needed it. My pitching arm was **ON FIRE**.

Johnny was right: how could Coach Hollylighter not see all I would bring to the team?

When we started running laps at the end of practice,

though, I got the sense that the other players were hanging back. "Come on, guys," I yelled, leading the pack.

But still, they lagged behind me. And they were chatting among themselves. Could they really have been that slow?

I was hoping they'd be inspired. Oh well.

I stayed out ahead of the team. It was never too late to inspire them. Running was a fundamental. When we were on our third lap, Coach Hollylighter called me over to her. This was it. This was when I'd officially join the team.

I jogged up and waited expectantly to hear how happy she'd sound.

"Hi, Coach! Team looks great out there, doesn't it?" I was kind of exaggerating. They were pretty slow.

"So I have some reservations," she said, not really answering my question. Out of the corner of my eye, I saw Johnny watching the conversation. I couldn't read his face but I wondered if this wasn't what he'd expected to hear, either.

Reservations? About what? I didn't say this out loud but my head wanted me to.

"We all know you're a good player," she said.

That was more like it.

"But . . ."

But??

"But our team has a good rapport, and I'm concerned about your ego," she said.

Ego? What ego? I have almost **NO EGO**. If you could look at me in an x-ray and actually see things like egos, mine would take up less room than my appendix. I'm not sure how big my appendix is but I know I don't need it for survival, so I'm guessing it's small. And my ego—if it even exists—is way, way smaller than my very unnecessary appendix.

OTHER THINGS WAY BIGGER THAN MY EGO

• A flattened dime

• A pencil eraser

• A sea monkey (no, I've never even seen one and that's my exact point)

• A baby's eyelash

• Molecules of small things

"I have lots of rapport. I can make rapport wherever I go," I started saying, really fast. I wasn't sure exactly what "rapport" was but I was sure I could make it. I wanted to play baseball so badly and **BRING** more winning **BACK** to my life that I was sure I could make an **APPENDIX** if I had to. And then throw it away because no one needs them.

"We'll have to see," Coach Hollylighter said as she patted me on the shoulder, like she felt really bad for me. Like I had to get my appendix and my ego removed with painful surgeries. "Let's see how it goes."

This all sounded so sad to me that I said, "See how what goes?"

"You, on the team," she said. "With reservations."

I knew what she meant, but to me, reservations are something you make in advance and have to wait for. And I'm sick of waiting.

WINS: 1
LOSSES: 4

I'm on a streak all right. Just the wrong kind . . .

PRACTICE MAKES IMPERFECT

Goal: Have rapport with my new team. (I looked it up and it means "a close and harmonious relationship in which people or groups understand each other and communicate well." I can do that!)

Action: Be the opposite of movie-moment/expert Gabby and instead be kind/ego-free Gabby who accepts her new role with grace and reaches out to her new teammates with love and understanding.

Post-Day Analysis:
April 24

Framing. I decided that was what I needed to do with myself. The way a catcher frames a pitch can mean the difference between whether an ump calls it a strike or a ball. It's the same pitch, but it's all about perspective.

And the way I framed myself mattered. I thought showing my superstar side was the way to go, but that's not the case with Coach Hollylighter.

Nope, this transition to Piper Bell had not been easy. I really thought that because I had a rep for being a **GREAT BALLPLAYER**, I'd just click into place, like a Lego or a missing puzzle piece or something. The baseball team would ask me to be on it, the other players would become my friends, and everything else would just start to work out. An easy win. "No problem," as my dad liked to say when he had to throw together an extra plate of food if someone just dropped by and he invited them to stay for dinner.

I mean, when Michael Jordan, my dad's favorite basketball player, came out of retirement and went to the Washington Wizards, that team was really excited. When Babe Ruth got traded from the Boston Red Sox to the Yankees, the Yankees were beyond excited. (And the Red Sox were so wrong to let him go that they were **CURSED** for years!)

I'd been having such a **PERFECT** year at Luther that it seemed like I would have the same momentum—that I would come to Piper Bell and just pick up where I left off at my old school.

But it hasn't been like that at all.

At Luther, I was a leader. I was the person you came to for help. I was a big deal.

And even though I have what's called a "big personality," I feel like it's not working for me here.

Sure, I'm on the team, but with **RESERVATIONS**.

I didn't expect a parade or anything, but I don't think anyone has ever had reservations about me, either. (And this time, by "reservations" I mean those feelings a person gets that mean they're not quite sure about you. Which might be worse than the reservations you make and wait for—because at least you get to stay at a hotel or eat food at the end of those. These reservations were just . . . yucky.)

And they were giving me a case of the yips. Old Me, in case you don't remember, the yips are what you call it when you get so nervous or so in your head about the game that you forget how to play, or at least how to do certain things. Like maybe you just start not being able to make the throw to first base. Or you try to throw a pitch you've thrown a million times, and you just hurl the ball at the dirt.

Or you realize that you had rapport with your old team all along but now that you learned what it means, you're not sure you'll have it with another team ever again.

And that means the yips just get worse, and you will probably forget how to even walk out onto the field.

I didn't think it had gotten that bad yet, but when I woke up this morning, I couldn't remember what arm I throw with. That would be like if you were an awesome speller or something and you suddenly forgot how to spell your name, or **CAT**. Or you're normally great at math and someone asks you what 10 plus 10 is and you say, "8,000" or "orange."

OTHER "YIPS" SITUATIONS

TO BE OR NOT TO BE... FINE WITH ME!

WE SHOULD PROBABLY WALK...

E = MC?

E EQUALS MC... I DUNNO!

I had to do better today.

So I was going to go to practice and be just what the Coach and my teammates needed: humble, helpful Gabby. Rapport Gabby. No Reservations Gabby. Reframed Gabby.

In the locker room after school, I put on my Piper Bell Penguins practice jersey for the first time in my entire life. In the mirror, the red and black colors looked strange. Luther Lion colors are gold and brown.

KNOWS SHE IS AN *ACE* PITCHER BUT DOESN'T MAKE A BIG DEAL ABOUT IT

>LISTENS< TO ALL COACH AND TEAMMATE DIRECTION

SMILES A LOT

WALKS ONE FOOT AT A TIME

NO "SWAGGER"

Devon and some of the other girls didn't wait for me after they changed. I was feeling down enough on myself that I didn't totally blame them. The sporting thing to do ("sporting," the old-people way for saying "nice") was to welcome your new teammate, but maybe that would be weird for them after I gave one of them a bloody nose and tried to boss everyone around. Neither of which I'd meant to do, but it didn't seem like anyone cared to learn my explanations.

But even though I got it, when the other girls left me alone in the locker room, I was in full yips mode.

And they were the worst kind of yips. Not just sporty yips, like how to throw or what hand I used; yips like "Is my shirt on right?"

I finally made my feet work and got out to the field. I checked the stands for Johnny but he wasn't there today, which made me feel even worse because he'd been the only person to say I belonged there. I knew I belonged there, but it was nice to have backup. And thumbs-ups.

But then Coach Hollylighter actually told me to go to the mound for the catch drill. Devon and the other pitchers stayed in the bull pen to practice. I was surprised Coach would let me lead stuff on the field.

It was what I wanted, but all of a sudden I wished I could be doing something else. It seemed like it would have been better to be part of the bull-pen festivities. The mound felt lonely.

Reframing wasn't working. I already felt so far outside the strike zone that I didn't think they could make a frame big enough to find me.

Three in-and-out breaths. A hand clap. My thing.

I kicked off the drill, throwing the ball first to Ryder at catcher, who was supposed to throw to first, who'd then throw to second, who'd throw to left, who'd throw to third, and on and on. Catch drills are usually fun and easy.

Except today when the ball came back my way, I saw it, but my arm stopped moving. I said, "Got it!" But then I didn't lift my arm and it sailed right over my head.

Oh.

No.

THE YIPS.

If they looked like anything, they'd be little monsters with mean faces, pinching me.

IS DEVON BETTER THAN ME?

Or maybe just a bunch of little hyperactive Gabbys running around inside my head, all freaking out about a different thing.

But I picked up the ball and threw it to the next player. I told the yips to go away. Somehow, I made it through the rest of catch even though my stomach felt twitchy and I was pinchy all over with the yips.

DO I LOOK WEIRD. IN RED AND BLACK?

Then Coach Hollylighter said I could pitch to batting practice.

AM I ACTING TOO SURE OF MYSELF?

I'M GOING TO FLUNK OUT OF THIS PLACE!

Okay, **PITCHING**, my specialty. I could do this. I *would* do this. I pitched great yesterday. Just, today, I wouldn't boss anyone around. I'd just pitch like the pitcher I knew I could be. The pitcher I know I am.

Yips, begone!!

When Madeleine stepped up to bat first, though, and she had a big pink Band-Aid across the top of her nose, I got shaky again. The little Gabby-yips went crazy: "What if I hit her?" "She's going to think I have it out for her!" "There's going to be more blood!" "The school will think I'm a serial killer, not just a Luther Polluter."

I threw a fastball that wasn't even fast. The way I threw it, it didn't even seem like much of a ball.

Also, it was chin music—high and inside. And to be honest, I'm unsure it was even a pitch. It was like trying to throw a feather. They're so light, they just kind of give up and blow back with the wind. It was close to being that. If a ball could shrug, mine did that.

But still, Madeleine jumped away from the plate.

"What, are you trying to kill me? What did I even do to **YOU**??"

She was being a little dramatic, since my pitch had all the

force behind it of a marshmallow, but I understood why she was skeptical.

Ryder tossed the ball back to me and I was relieved to catch it. Which was all wrong, since I usually didn't even think about catching. Catching is like breathing. You just do it. You don't get excited when it happens, just worried when it doesn't.

"I'm sorry, I'm sorry," I said to Madeleine. She was staring at me like she was trying to memorize my face for a police sketch. "Let me try again."

But Madeleine stepped away from the plate.

"Coach, permission to skip batting practice?"

Coach Hollylighter shook her head. "It was one pitch," she said. Ah, thank goodness, my coach has faith in me! "Stay at bat. Gabby needs the practice."

Needs the practice????

Okay: I've heard plenty of things about myself. "Gabby practices hard!" or "You can tell she practices a lot."

But "needs the practice" was new. Just like someone "having reservations" about me. She knew about my Luther stats! I didn't need the practice. Ugh.

Suddenly, I felt extra-twitchy all over. But I had to prove that I was worth having around. And I definitely didn't want to argue with Coach Hollylighter.

So I didn't say anything. And I told the little Gabby-yips,

who were kicking up dirt and making a lot of noise about that practice comment, to **CALM DOWN**.

I threw another pitch. It was a good one. Humble, needs-the-practice Gabby could still pitch.

Madeleine bunted. To me. Who bunted in batting practice????

But I grabbed the ball and tossed it to first, where Mario Salamida was waiting.

It didn't matter that he was there, though, because it went sailing right over his massive head.

"What was that, Gaggy?" Mario yelled. "Are you sure you've ever even played this game before?"

"Salamida, we don't talk to our teammates like that!" Coach Hollylighter said, making me feel a bit better. Then she blew the whistle and called me in. She told the players on the field to keep playing. I thought Mario, who was not being very rapport-like, should have gotten benched for a bit, but I wasn't the one in charge.

I jogged over to Coach Hollylighter, trying to look yips-free.

"You okay, Garcia?"

I nodded. "Yes, just getting used to things." Over her shoulder, I could see Devon and the other players in the bull pen slowing down, probably trying to overhear us.

I thought she looked concerned when she said, "I know

you have skills. We'll give it some time so you can adjust."

One of my little Gabby-yips was happy that she commented on my skills. But the rest were wondering what she thought I needed to adjust.

Has anyone ever had a case of the yips for their **WHOLE LIFE**?

Another **LOSS**, with a side of **YIPS**.

WINS: 1 (with reservations)
LOSSES: 5

April 25
Replay: Game One

How can I say this without sounding negative?

My first game as a Piper Bell Penguin was **THE WORST GAME OF MY LIFE**.

WORST.

GAME.

OF.

MY.

LIFE.

I refuse to write an inning-by-inning summary because I hated every inning.

"Hated every inning" are three words I never thought I'd

put together. But there they are. And they are **TRUE**.

It was an out-of-conference game against the Dalton Dynamite, so not as crucial as if the team had been in Piper Bell's conference. But I'd played the Dynamite earlier in the season with Luther, whose conference they were in. Now, since Luther had no team because there was no school until the asbestos thing got fixed, all the teams in Luther's conference were playing these out-of-conference games. But all this is to say, I know the Dynamite aren't very good. We'd won easily.

Piper Bell should have won easily, too.

I was pretty excited going in to the game. Practice the day after my yips practice had gone better. Not rapport better, but I didn't make any major mistakes. Devon and I both spent time in the bull pen, and we even talked a little.

Devon: Do you ever feel like baseball is your real life and the rest of your life is just the game part? Or like when you win a game, you win at everything?

Me: That is how I feel all. the. time.

Devon: Yeah, I can tell that about you.

Then she blinked and stopped talking and lobbed a fastball at Ryder. She was like one of those cowboys in old movies who say just the perfect thing and then get glinty-eyed and go back to their horse. Personally, I think those movies all seem the same, but Peter and my dad love them and claim each one is very special. But they all have the glinty-eyed cowboy.

Anyway, even if she was a little scary, it felt something like rapport to be talking to Devon.

So, after that more promising practice, game day. All the signs were there that this would be the true, official start of my **NEW WINNING STREAK**. The winning streak I just kept waiting for.

THE SIGNS

- **Sky:** Clear.

- **Ponytail:** No shark fin.

- **Breakfast:** Chocolate chip pancakes.

These things were all signs of a universe that wanted me to be happy. And a **WIN** would make me very happy.

Plus, the win would be at **BASEBALL**! I was due.

That's kind of superstitious but I did the math: I'd been denied the rightful win I had coming on asbestos day, and that's when everything started going downhill. So a baseball win now would put the cosmos in order and make things okay.

The stands were full, the field was mowed. Everything would be great.

Maybe a little part of me thought I would be pitching. So when Coach Hollylighter told Devon she was starting and I might be called in as a reliever, well, I admit it, I wasn't in love with the idea.

I think Coach saw my pouty face because she said, "That a problem, Garcia?"

"No, that's great! Of course, it's perfect!" I was really over-selling it but since my ego was a concern, I had to.

And instead, I decided to be **SUPER-SUPPORTIVE**. If I could get Devon to really like me, I could win Coach Hollylighter over, too. So, in the bull pen while Devon warmed up, I tried to be helpful.

Me: You know, I played these guys before. Their best batter can't hit a slider at all.

Devon: Oh, really? That's interesting.

But she said it like it was not interesting at all. Maybe it wasn't to her. Or maybe Devon, in addition to her scary-cowboy talk, was a total game-face athlete. My hero, Mo'Ne Davis, is like that, too: sometimes even when the game is going totally her way, you can't tell from her expression.

I'm a little more like Julie Johnston, a defender on the U.S.

World Cup soccer team: when a game is going good, she's all smiles. Both ways work. But I thought Devon could at least crack a small smile.

Why did I have to do all the work building rapport? What about everyone else? And why did it seem like just when rapport got started, it stopped?

So I tried again as Devon headed for the mound and I sat in the dugout. "Go get 'em, DeWitt," I said, and I smiled really big. Not in a fake way, either, even though on the inside, I **REALLY REALLY REALLY** wanted to pitch. (Because I **REALLY REALLY REALLY** wanted to win.)

"Thanks, dude," she said, and slapped me five as she headed to the mound. Dude. She called me dude. Things were moving back in the right direction.

Or so I thought.

HIGHLIGHT (BUT REALLY LOWLIGHT) REEL

Inning 1: Normal enough. Devon was throwing good stuff. The team was playing fine, maybe not Luther Lions fine but good enough.

Inning 2: The opponents scored a run when their best hitter got Devon's curve. And then another couple. (She should have tried a slider.) But we scored a few runs. Tie.

Inning 4: Devon asked me for advice: "So the slider, you think that will work? I wanna bust this guy." She had total game face. I had total happy face because she was asking me for help: "Yeah, there's no way it won't work."

Inning 4, a few minutes later: The guy homered off Devon's first pitch. Her slider. **THIS WAS NOT GOOD.**

Inning 5: Devon was falling apart on the mound. And **TOTALLY BLAMED ME**. "You just wanted to pitch," she said, looking like she might growl.

"No, that's not it at all! I swear, the guy usually can't hit a slider, at least not mine."

"Ugh, Gaggy, give it a rest with the bragging," Mario said, patting Devon on the shoulder.

And everyone seemed to feel sorry for Devon, like my advice just ruined her life. But it wasn't my fault!

Inning 6: Coach said she was going to put me in. This was good, even if I was worried Devon would be angry. She was already angry.

It was also when I could make or break myself. I folded the sides of my mitt one-two, one-two, making the sides touch.

"You're going in?" Johnny said from the bench, where he'd been manning the score book.

I smiled, **BIG**, but checked to make sure not too many people saw it, like I was happy for Devon's mess-up. "Seems like it!"

"Sweet, you'll be great," Johnny said, and gave me a thumbs-up. His thumbs-ups had a way of making me feel pretty good.

Until Madeleine sauntered by, getting a cup of water. "You're pitching?"

I nodded. "Yup!"

"Well, I hope they have strong noses." She was never going to get over that.

But that made me think of all that blood gushing from her face and then . . .

Between Devon's anger and the visions of blood, I started to sweat. Then I pictured the whole Dalton Dynamite team just coming at me like bleeding zombies (do zombies bleed or do they ooze?).

And then, the yips.

Yup, the yips were **BACK**.

Just as Coach Hollylighter went to the mound to tell Devon I was coming in.

Devon came out and huffed past me, "Good luck out there," but not in a voice that meant it at all. "Hope that slider works for **YOU**."

Because the Dalton batter who'd homered on Devon was up again.

And I had the **YIPS**.

Then I looked right at the batter's face and I knew he knew I was going to throw the slider.

What happened next was awful. I didn't throw a slider. Nope. I threw a meatball.

A meatball—the biggest, juiciest, easiest-to-hit pitch imaginable. And my pitch was such a giant meatball that I might as well have been standing on a huge plate of spaghetti.

Ugh, I knew the batter was going to take such a big bite out of that stupid meatball. My legs felt like spaghetti standing on a pile of spaghetti.

Crack!!

The hit was a perfect line drive to center, not

MEATBALL THE EASIEST PITCHES TO HIT...

a high fly ball but just high enough to whiz right over my head. It was up to Madeleine to catch it.

For a second, I imagined she was going to jump out of the way, since everything I do injures her somehow. But she was running for it, and she dove with her glove stretched out in front of her and snagged the ball out of midair.

If Madeleine hadn't been there, it could have been a lot worse.

But it didn't matter. Every pitch I threw after that was a nightmare. Everything was awful. And the team that was waiting for me in the dugout was not one that I had any rapport with.

We lost. Stats-wise, the loss went to Devon. But all my hopes for starting a new win streak were ruined.

It got worse.

I was packing my equipment bag quietly. None of us were talking. It was the Penguins' first loss, after all. I looked around for someone to talk to and tell me it was no big deal, but even Johnny Madden, who I thought was a fan, or my friend, or something, was quiet. He gave me the saddest of smiles and said, "You know, it's not a big deal." But it was a big deal. The biggest. I could tell he knew it. He'd been my first fan and I'd let him down. I'd let everyone down. The first game I played in and the Penguins' winning streak was no more.

AND THEN I heard Devon say to Mario, "We should have won that game."

And Mario said, "Yeah, it's all Gaggy's fault."

And Devon said, "Is it her fault she's a **JINX**??"

A **JINX**????

A **JINX** is worse than a **LOSER**. A jinx not only loses but rains down losing on everything around them.

FAMOUS SPORTS JINXES AND CURSES

- **Billy Goat Curse:** The reason why the Chicago Cubs hadn't won a World Series between 1908 and 2016. They failed at their last chance in 1945, when the owner of the Billy Goat Tavern put a curse on the team after he was told to leave a World Series game because his pet goat was too smelly to bring to the ballpark. (But now you can't even bring a water bottle to the ballpark, so it seems like he was getting away with a lot.)

- **Madden Cover Curse:** It's said that whatever NFL player is on the cover of this video game (which is no relation to Johnny Madden) will get hurt, have a bad season, or quit.

- **Heisman Trophy Curse:** Another football one. Whatever college player wins the Heisman screws up in bowl games or is just no good when they're recruited by pro teams.

- **Sports Illustrated Cover Jinx:** Athletes who get the cover of the magazine often are injured or lose important games after appearing on it. It happened to my all-time fave, Mo'Ne Davis. After she was the first girl to ever throw a shutout game in the Little League World Series, she lost a crucial game to Chicago, ending her team's championship run.

JINXES ARE REAL! AND NOW I'M A REAL-LIFE JINX!

I wouldn't want to play with a jinx, no offense to the jinxes of the world.

WINS 1: (but probably a lie)
LOSSES: 6 (times a thousand because I'm a JINX)

WITS ABOUT YOU

Post-Day Analysis:
April 26

The Wits About You is a **SURPRISE** play. It happens in base-ball, a lot. Like, I can't always necessarily strategize or plan because I don't know what's going to happen. Maybe a batter who always swings for the fences suddenly bunts. Or a ball looks like it's going to make it over the outfield wall for a homer but it stops just short and I can make a diving catch.

To be prepared for these plays, I need my wits about me: to be alert, observant, ready for anything. Like a lion ready to strike. (Except lions sleep 20 hours a day, so they only have their wits about them for four hours a day. Lazy.)

So there I was, the day after the lousiest lousy game I've ever played. I was a jinx. I wanted to quit everything.

JINX EVIDENCE:

- On the way into school, I tried to hold the door for some eighth graders but smashed the door into Ms. Pluhar's face because I didn't see her standing there.

- In English class, everyone who was sitting near me had pens that ran out of ink.

- My shoes came untied, and when I went to retie them, the laces snapped. On both.

- Of the three people who actually smiled at me today, all three of them had stuff in their teeth and didn't hear me when I tried to tell them.

Being a jinx made me feel not like myself. I did not like feeling not like myself. **I LIKE MYSELF**. Other people like myself. Diego called me a force of positivity, even when we were arguing about something. I used to get bonus french fries and invites to every birthday party. I had a cheering section. Now I was a colossal bummer.

I didn't even know if I should go to practice. Devon hated me, and Mario already hated me, and Madeleine was scared of me. Johnny was disappointed in me. And Coach Hollylighter had never wanted me on the team in the first place. So, pretty much, I had the opposite of rapport.

At lunch, I avoided the baseball team and went to one of Piper Bell's "atriums." They're just big, glass-windowed rooms that get superhot, so most students steer clear of them. Except me and Johnny Madden, it turned out.

Of course, his face was buried in a textbook. And I still felt so lame for him witnessing my jinxiness that I started to turn around—maybe I could find a supply closet to sit in and eat my lunch.

"Hey, Gabby," he said. Darn. I couldn't just walk out now.

"Hey," I said, and sat down with my history textbook, opening my lunch sack on the small table next to me. I didn't say anything else because I couldn't think of anything. So I flipped through my book. Somehow I'd become a person who ate lunch quietly reading my history textbook. (I was pretending to read it. I hoped I wouldn't find out Louie was wrong about that "no real letter grades" thing, because I hadn't exactly been focusing on my studies. It's a hard thing to do when you're having an identity crisis.)

But I ate my turkey sandwich (switched from a Tupperware container of mushy leftover enchiladas that Dumpster had eaten in seconds) and stared at facts about the Revolutionary War.

"How's it going?"

I looked up and saw that Johnny Madden was talking to me.

"That game was awful, huh? I really jinxed everyone."

I didn't even try to make some kind of pleasant conversation because—Hey! Jinx over here—and who cared what a jinx had to say? Plus, it was the only thing on my mind.

"It wasn't all your fault," he said. "The whole jinx idea is stupid."

"You don't believe in jinxes?"

"Mathematically, no. The team was due to have an off game and it just happened to coincide with your arrival."

"Sounds like a jinx to me."

"Or just randomness and chance and some errors," he said. "I think you're being too hard on yourself." He leaned back over his books then, and even though I didn't feel better, I was glad at least one person wasn't completely against me. Maybe I hadn't disappointed him too badly.

"Thanks," I said. I wanted to ask him something else, but I couldn't think of anything good. Instead, I managed to read a whole chapter of my history book and finish my sandwich before the bell rang for the next period.

I was surprised when Johnny waited for me at the atrium entryway. "I'll walk with you to algebra." He was brave, to be willing to be seen with a jinx.

As we walked down the hall, my thoughts bounced back and forth: 1. I was a jinx. 2. Did Johnny **LIKE** me?

Why else would he be trying to reassure me by talking about how even so-called bad professional players are still pretty good overall because statistically they might only get on base two out of every ten at bats but all told blah blah blah . . . I wanted to listen, I did. He was smart and kind of interesting and I got the sense that not many people listened to him. But I was having a problem staying focused.

Whatever Johnny's deal was, I believe in jinxes as much as I believe in math. They are **FACT**. And they've probably been around longer than math, when I think about it.

"Besides," he was saying, "there's no such thing really as a perfect season. Unless you're not playing. But then you're not doing anything."

He was a little right on that, but shouldn't a person **AIM** for a perfect season? And not be a **JINX**? I wasn't about to argue with Johnny's math, but I still thought that if I was a jinx, I'd ruin the baseball team. And they had had a perfect season, until me.

I was sure I would never feel like a winner again. Baseball was my sport, right? I needed to make it work for me, didn't I? But how did I do that when everything was just not working?

I still had no plan when I walked into algebra the next period. The classroom was **CHAOS**. All the thinking I was doing was taken over by just trying to process what was going on.

And then I understood: we had a substitute.

It was Coach Raddock, who the school called a "floating sub." Which makes me think of a ghostly submarine, but I don't come up with these crazy names. Coach Raddock was the opposite of Coach Hollylighter, at least appearance-wise. She was short, with a fuzzy puff of curls pulled on top of her head and the kind of face that looked like she was always about to smile. Even now, when things weren't going well.

COACH RADDOCK FLOATING ABOVE THE CLASS

The class was not being kind to Coach Raddock. To be honest, a ghost submarine would have gotten their attention way better.

No one was in their seats. And the reason came down to Mario and some of his goon squad. They were batting around Mr. Patler's Albert Einstein action figure from one end of the room to the other, trying to get him into the wastebaskets on either side of the room.

Meanwhile, the other students were cheering and jumping around like crazy, counting how many times Albert flew back and forth. (The action figure, not the real Einstein. I would hope the true discoverer of relativity would get more respect.)

Coach Raddock was at the front of the classroom, waving around Mr. Patler's lesson plan, saying, "Look, I don't know what you all ate for lunch today, but we have work to do."

She saw me and I guess she knew who I was because she said, "Garcia, can you please erase the board?"

In that moment, I knew I had a choice.

I could join in with everyone else in the Einstein game. Or I could do what Coach Raddock had asked. She knew my name and was being nice to me. I should go with Coach Raddock.

So I stepped up to the whiteboard and started to scrub away the marker from a few days ago. I finally managed to conquer a stubborn equation and was about to put the eraser down and go to my seat, even as the other chaos took place around me.

But then Albert Einstein came flying at my head. Tiny action-figure Albert, just to be clear, but he was **FAST**. Before I knew what was happening, I swatted him away with the eraser and he traveled directly to the wastebasket behind Mario, whose head swiveled as he watched the toy cruise by.

Albert landed with a clunk in the trash basket and the whole room burst into applause.

After the game the day before, and yeah, everything else, it felt really good. Good and very unjinx-like.

Mario, of course, was sulking about it. But then he got his mean-Mario face on and said, "Too bad your reflexes don't work on the field, Gaggy."

Which didn't even make sense, because it wasn't like my reflexes had been bad in the game. It was just that everything I did had been bad.

"Too bad your brain doesn't work anywhere, Mario." It wasn't the insult he deserved, but it was an answer.

"Calm, calm," Coach Raddock said, but she looked relieved that the Mario and Gabby trash-talk session had somehow quieted the class. Then she looked at me. "That was a nice goal, Gabby—like someone who plays field hockey."

Wait. Field hockey.

Hmm, field hockey.

Was Coach Raddock telling me I should think about field hockey?

Of course she was, after that goal.

But I'm a baseball player, I thought. Through and through, forever and always.

Well, I *was* a baseball player. I wasn't sure I was really much of one lately. **JINX JINX JINX**, the tiny Gabbys cried as announcers Bob and Judy just held their heads in their hands.

But then . . .

Whoa. *I was going to think about field hockey.* I **NEEDED** to think about field hockey. Maybe that was what I should have been doing all along. If my sport wasn't working, maybe I needed to change it.

As we took our seats, Johnny Madden said, "She's right; the field hockey team is pretty weak. Statistically speaking, one good player would make a huge difference. One good player would be 100 percent more good players than that team has."

A huge difference?

Like a **BEST-SEASON-EVER** difference?

I could imagine it all now, me, Gabby Garcia, single-handedly changing the fate of the doomed team. A doomed team with a coach who had—kind of—suggested I join, like I was **WANTED**. For my **WINNING** abilities.

Maybe the solution to my jinxiness wasn't waiting for a bunch of math-y statistics to turn in my favor.

Maybe it was accepting my field hockey **FATE**.

WIN!

WINS: 2
LOSSES: 6 (that's starting to look better already!)

FIELD HOCKEY FANTASTIC

Goal: Try to be awesome at my new sport and make the team.
Action: Play hard, don't be full of myself, and try my best at a totally new sport I've never played!

Post-Day Analysis:
April 29

So I felt like Michael Jordan. I'm usually on the Mo'Ne Davis trajectory but today I can't not think about Michael, "Air" Jordan, my dad's favorite athlete. Dad said there's no one better. He won't shut up about it.

But once upon a time, Michael Jordan switched sports.

He tried to play baseball.

Here's the thing: Michael Jordan is an elite athlete.

But he was not elite at all at baseball.

THINGS MICHAEL JORDAN HAS PROBABLY NEVER DONE THAT HE WAS PROBABLY BETTER AT THAN BASEBALL

- Tightrope walking

- Giving guided tours of museums devoted to strange things, like eating utensils or birdcages

- Being quizzed on the Dewey decimal system

- Making butter from scratch like they do in Colonial Williamsburg

So who knew what was going to happen with me and field hockey? I mean, I **WANTED** to be good. I expected that I could be good. And, from what I'd heard, the field hockey team was not that good. So I could be the best person on a bad team, maybe? Or maybe make the team good? I would love to make a bad team good.

But first I needed to know something about field hockey. There was only one person for that: Diego. And, as luck would have had it, we'd been scheduled for a phone call night. So, after he told me that jungle life was getting lonely and we counted the days up until he was supposed to be back (forty-two, if all went as planned—and there happened to be an Atlanta Braves home game the day after he returned, so we decided to go), I told him about my **JINX** status and about my field hockey plans.

He'd been skeptical at first. "But you're a **BASEBALL PLAYER**. The best one I know."

"But I think the universe is trying to tell me something, Diego. Maybe I need to try this. As part of my story."

(Diego loves athlete life stories, especially ones with twists and turns. Michael Jordan didn't make his high school varsity basketball team when he first tried out, for example. Joe DiMaggio and Ted Williams were great baseball players who missed seasons in the prime of their careers because they were called to military service. My girl Mo'Ne Davis actually thinks of herself as a basketball player first, and a baseball player second, even though she's clearly awesome at baseball.)

And Diego came through.

Today in every class, I peeked inside my books, where I'd hidden a printout of some field hockey guidelines Diego had drawn up over the weekend.

There was a personal note on the top:

I know it sounds great to be surrounded by adorable monkeys all day but let me tell you, it's not. Monkeys are

not all that nice. Not one monkey has climbed up sweetly on my shoulder and nuzzled my ear, like monkeys do on TV. But you know how you've heard they throw poop? Yeah, they definitely do that.

The note made me feel a little better because I felt a little like poop had been thrown at me since I got here. Only it was Piper Bell Penguin poop and also not actual poop. Okay, fine, maybe Diego has it worse. Actual poop was definitely worse than poop of my imagination.

But his **FIELD HOCKEY BASICS** were:

- Eleven players on the field (usually in arrangements of three forwards, three midfielders, four defenders, and a goalkeeper)

- A lot of running and a lot of "fluidity" (which means, that, unlike in baseball where a first baseman stays at first base, a forward might end up defending, etc.)

- Carry the stick to your right side at all times

• Can only score from within the striking circle

• Basically ice hockey but on grass and more fancy

He sent me a bunch of videos and guides online that I watched and read last night, but you can watch and watch and read and read and watch and it is no substitute for playing. Diego himself is truly the biggest sports expert I know but he's **TERRIBLE** at sports. (Sorry, Diego, but you won't see this: it's a super-secret playbook, even to you.)

So I was extra-nervous when I walked out onto the field hockey pitch where I was told to try out. I'd never even been on a "pitch" before.

It was weird that I pitched on a baseball field but would play field hockey on a pitch.

Anyway!

I also sensed the little Gabbys getting fired up about things. All of them were more nervous than I was.

What if I made a complete idiot of myself out there?

But when I got to where I thought I was supposed to go, I just found a bunch of kids doing yoga. Not even the kind of yoga you could confuse for rigorous stretching but, like, "sit with your legs crossed and eyes closed and breathe deep" yoga.

I looked around for Coach Raddock. Maybe practice got moved.

It was mesmerizing, all these students so quiet and still. I recognized a few. Katy Harris, who was in my bio class and was a singer who performed her original songs on a hit YouTube channel. (Also the subject of the untrue rumor that I got her sick on my first day here.) And this girl Molly Oliver, an eighth grader who always carried around books that weren't schoolbooks. I heard she wrote a novel. And Colin Reedy, a very quiet boy from my social studies class—or a boy who would be quiet if he didn't wear his tap shoes everywhere.

I was definitely in the wrong place. This must have been Yoga Club.

Someone tapped me on the shoulder. Coach Raddock.

Thank goodness! She was here to take me to the right place.

"Hi, Gabby," she said. "How are you? I'm so glad you're here." She was talking in a soft, peaceful voice. A much more Zen voice than she was using in algebra yesterday, but maybe it was because she was surrounded by the yoga fest. It was so calming. Like watching a sheep's fur grow.

OTHER CALMING THINGS

- Koalas nibbling eucalyptus

- Very organized store clerks folding sweaters

- Steam rising from boiling pots of noodles

- The first blob of ketchup flowing out of the bottle

"Where am I?" That was what I said, and my voice sounded odd, like someone asking an alien life-form what planet they've woken up on. But I kind of felt that way.

"You're on the field hockey pitch." Now it was Coach Raddock's turn to sound odd. She even answered like she was the leader of beings from another dimension.

"Is this field hockey?" I must have spoken too loudly because she held a finger up to her lips for me to be quieter. Then she nodded.

"Game tomorrow. We like to take it easy the day before a game. We need to be quiet as the team gets into the proper head space."

Okay, so taking it easy the day before a game wasn't that strange. But this seemed beyond easy. It was like sleeping. And from what Johnny Madden said, the team needed work, not sleep.

"So maybe I should practice with the team before playing in a game?"

She waved her hand through the air like this was the craziest suggestion she'd ever heard. "Nah, why wait? You look like you're a size small. I'll get you a uniform. You can play tomorrow."

What? Was my garbage-can goal enough to just get on the pitch? And, wait, if I thought about it, Coach Raddock didn't say I should try out for field hockey. She didn't even say that I should play field hockey. All she said was that I made the goal *like someone who plays field hockey.*

But, looking around at her team and based on what Johnny said, I wondered if she'd ever seen anyone actually play field hockey.

"So I'm on the team?"

She nodded. "You're welcome to sit in on the last of yoga. Or you can just watch."

It was the weirdest tryout or practice or whatever I'd ever been to. But at least she didn't have reservations about me.

I looked around for a hidden camera.

Or a portal to another dimension.

Maybe I was already in one?

I guess I "made" the team, so . . . **WIN?**

WINS: 3
LOSSES: 6 (if I keep this up, I'll be close to .500!)

LAST CHANCE

Goal: Be a field hockey player?
Action: Quit the baseball team.

April 29,
Part Two

Okay, I made the team. But I hadn't really *made* the team. Is it really a tryout if you don't have to try?

Still, I just stopped to write this in the sweaty atrium after wandering the halls, carrying around a brand-new field hockey uniform after a supportive pat on the back from Coach Raddock and instructions to be ready for tomorrow's game. When I asked how to be ready, she said, "You are probably already ready. Readiness comes from within."

But doesn't readiness also come from having some idea of what you're going to do?

It's all very confusing. I'm very disoriented. Suddenly, I'm unsure I **WANT** to be on the team.

If it was that easy to get on, is it a good place to be?

Sure it is. Coach Raddock is nice and there's nothing wrong with yoga. Something doesn't have to be competitive to be worthwhile, or to put me back on my win streak. (And that makes me think about an assignment about irony that I keep putting off in English class.)

At any rate, I'm on the field hockey team and will have to quit the baseball team. I've never really quit anything before. I'm not even sure how you do that. And now I'm sweating for more reasons than just the atrium.

I'm probably already on Coach Hollylighter's Poop List for being so late for practice. Or maybe—

What if I make the competition about **ME**?

A play is taking shape in my brain.

New Goal: SEEM like I am going to be a field hockey player.

New Action: Quit the baseball team while announcing my field hockey plans.

Secret Goal: See if Coach Hollylighter will ask me to stay on the baseball team.

It's just like when Peter complains that he doesn't want

whatever my dad makes for dinner and my dad offers to make him something else that Peter **REALLY** wouldn't want and then Peter admits that he's fine with what was originally offered. (The mind games required to keep Peter in the family are really troublesome.)

So here I am, starting to think I don't want to play field hockey. But I also don't want to go back to a baseball team that doesn't want me and thinks I'm a jinx. So, maybe, if the baseball team **BELIEVES** I want to leave, they'll be upset to lose me, and ask me to stay??

I think it's a great plan. I just need to change into this field hockey uniform.

A win is coming soon.

THE TAKE-ME-OUT
FAKE-OUT

Goal: Get baseball team to admit they want to keep me by making them think I am leaving.

Action: Convincingly act like I really want to quit the team to be a field hockey player.

Post-Play Analysis:
April 29, continued, AGAIN

With my new play in mind, I put on my new uniform in one of the school bathrooms. I looked in the mirror to check my face. I wanted to look serious and concerned and like I felt just **TERRIBLE** about this hard decision but that I knew it was the **RIGHT MOVE**. For **EVERYONE**.

Here is the face I settled on:

SUPER-SERIOUS,
DARK-NIGHT-OF-THE-SOUL
TYPE OF FACE

+ DRAMATIC,
IMAGINARY
WIND, OBVS

MY NEW
HOCKEY
STICK
EH.....

No one could not believe the deep spiritual crisis of a face like that. I mean, if I really thought the baseball team was just going to let me leave, the spiritual crisis would have been 100 percent real, so it wasn't too hard to fake it. Because I **REALLY** didn't want to leave baseball.

So I kept that face and that mood as I headed to the baseball field. I was anxious that Coach Hollylighter and the team would be worried about me or upset with me for missing practice. But when I got there, they were just on the field, practicing like I wasn't even gone. Or maybe like I was, and like they didn't even miss me.

Was I imagining things or did they look really happy?

They probably **WERE** happy, to be rid of a jinx.

Suddenly, standing there in my field hockey uniform, I knew I would rather be out on the field. The baseball field, not the field hockey pitch. I mean, how many hours had I spent on baseball fields? How many innings? How many baseball moments had I logged? A person didn't just let that kind of thing slide through their hands.

BUT . . .

I wanted the baseball team to be happy when I was actually on the field with them, not just on days I didn't show up for practice.

I stepped up behind Coach Hollylighter, who was standing on the first baseline talking to Coach Tommy, a college student who sometimes comes to practice as a batting coach.

I cleared my throat with one of those "hmmmh-hmmmh" noises and they both turned to look at me. Alongside the fence, Johnny was doodling some kind of ball-arc diagram that looked complicated but potentially interesting. He looked up and made a squinchy face when he saw my field hockey uniform.

"Gabby," Coach Hollylighter said. "We were wondering why you weren't here." I guessed that was nice, to at least be wondered about.

But everyone on the field kept playing as usual. Lee Castle, one of the other starting pitchers, who was only okay, was on the mound with Devon at bat. Ryder was at catcher. Coach Tommy headed to home plate to help Devon with something and left me with Coach Hollylighter.

Besides her and Johnny, I wasn't sure anyone else even registered my presence.

"Oh, yeah, about that," I started, wanting her to see my uniform and to say the rest so I didn't have to. And then I wanted her to say, "We don't want you to leave! You're gonna be great!" Pretending to quit the Piper Bell baseball team might have been worse than really trying to get on it. "Well, you see, I . . ."

All of the sudden, my dark-night-of-the-soul face felt very real. There was so much hinging on this moment: I needed to know that I wasn't a jinx and that the baseball team wanted me to stick around and knew I was a winner. But Coach Hollylighter was looking irritated and staring at me like she wished she had a tool to pull words out of my mouth. (And wouldn't that be a pretty helpful tool?)

the
"I-Hate-To-Say-This"
SUPER
WORD
EXTRACTOR

I hate to say this but....

CAN'T FIND THE WORDS?

WE'LL PULL THEM RIGHT OUT!

DIFFICULT NEWS YOU JUST HAVE TO BREAK?

THE WORD EXTRACTOR WILL BREAK IT FOR YOU!

ORDER NOW

"Have you joined the field hockey team?" she said, pointing at my uniform.

I looked down. I'd forgotten it was on. That probably was not a good sign for my enthusiasm. But, any minute, Coach Hollylighter would make sure I stuck with baseball.

"Yes," I started, trying to think of the very fancy way a big sports star would leave a team that had been very dear to him or her. Granted, the Penguins weren't exactly dear to me, or vice versa, but maybe I should have prepared a statement.

"It became clear at this juncture . . . ," I started, thinking that—**WHOA**, I definitely sounded important! "Well, this juncture made it clear that . . . okay, it was suggested that I might be good at field hockey team, so I tried out and I made the team. I think they see me as a valuable addition to their lineup and, even though baseball is the sport I'm meant to play, I felt this was a good decision."

My voice was shaky and I was looking at Coach Hollylighter hoping yet again for ESP, or whatever I needed so that she knew that I didn't really want to leave. *Readmymindreadmymindreadmymind*, I thought.

I caught Johnny's eye and he mouthed, with a crazed expression: "What are you doing??" But I ignored him. If it worked out, and it had to, he'd understand.

"I see," she said, and it was definitely in that grown-up way that sort of lets you know that the grown-up knows that maybe you are not telling the whole truth. But she didn't continue or say anything about me staying on the team or even hint that maybe things would get better. I was hoping for at least an "Are you sure about that?" But nothing.

"I've really enjoyed my time playing baseball," I tacked on, and it was such an understatement! *Really enjoyed* my time playing the sport that gives my life meaning? **NO**, I live and breathe baseball! Jinx or not, it was my game. But I didn't know how to say that. It didn't feel very winner-y.

And having started the whole thing, I didn't want to suddenly say, "Wait! I still want to play baseball! Even if you all hate me!"

And that part did stink. I wanted to be **APPRECIATED**.

The whole thing was a mess of words and thoughts and ideas and plays and strategies piled up in a jumble of wrong in the pit of my stomach. But I wasn't just going to take it all back!

"I'm sure you'll enjoy your days as a field hockey player, then, too," Coach Hollylighter said. "Of course, we all wish you the best of luck."

Huh? **THAT WASN'T WHAT SHE WAS SUPPOSED TO SAY!**

I felt myself shrinking into my new uniform, for a sport I'd never played. I heard the crack of the bat and saw Devon hit a nice line drive up the middle of the field. I almost clapped and cheered her on as she ran past me to first.

And then I remembered, I wasn't on the team anymore. So here I am, a baseball player without a team, with a field hockey uniform crumpled in a pile on her bedroom floor, writing about what might be the worst day of her life. The **NEW** worst day of her life.

Definitely a **LOSS**.

WINS: 3
LOSSES: 7

THINGS MY PARENTS SAID
WHEN I DECIDED TO QUIT BASEBALL

• "But baseball is your first love!"

• "Was someone mean to you?"

• "Do you feel okay? Do you need something to eat?"

• "Would chocolate help?"

• "Baseball is your sport! Are you sure about this?"

• "Let me take your temperature."

- "But you're such a great pitcher. You belong out there!"

- "Transitions are hard. Are you sure? Maybe you should give it more time."

- "Maybe it's puberty." (The official reason parents give for anything they can't explain once you're over twelve years old.)

- "Why field hockey? Have you ever **PLAYED** field hockey?"

- "You don't feel peer pressure, do you?"

- "Are you sure you're not just hungry?"

- "Maybe you should sleep on it."

- "Does she look flushed?"

- "I thought she looked pale."

- "Something's wrong. Where's the doctor's number?"

- "Okay, if you're really sure, we absolutely support you."

- "You can always go back to baseball, though."

- "Adolescence can be difficult. Lots of changes. Just give yourself room to breathe."

- "You can tell us anything."

- "Field hockey, huh? Well, it's never a dull moment with you."

- "I'll fix you something to eat."

FIRST GAME

Goal: Try to be awesome at my new sport, impress my new teammates, and single-handedly save the field hockey team.
Action: Get my team psyched. Talk plays, try to get a feel for my new sport, be the athlete I know I can be and **AM**.

Post-Day Analysis:
April 30

Okay, so this playbook is about **GOALS**.
ACTIONS.
RESULTS.
But the results I expect are never quite the results I get.
It's been driving me kind of nuts because, as a pitcher, I'm

almost always able to think about what I'm going to do and do it.

So I'm frustrated because I keep planning ways to be awesome at Piper Bell and get my record-settingly awesome life back, then they don't work out. It all counted on the baseball team thing as the center of the plan, but that team didn't want me.

THINGS THAT HAVE NOT WORKED OUT

- Getting a C in History (yup, progressive grades were just a rumor! I'd give anything for that sweatpants grading system now)

- Haven't made any friends except maybe a cute-type boy in a tie but it's weird, so . . .

- Not on the baseball team

- Shark-fin hair still not going away

- Somehow on the field hockey team (not necessarily a bad thing, but odd, definitely odd because **IT'S NOT THE BASEBALL TEAM**)

I would never have thought this outcome was possible. Me not playing baseball is weird. In my mind, me playing baseball is like a law of the universe. Like the ice cream truck showing up after you've just eaten ice cream.

Me quitting the baseball team is even stranger, like some alternate universe where instead of ice cream trucks, kids run up to trucks selling kale smoothies.

Quitting isn't something I do. But I haven't really quit, I don't think. Because I joined something else, and I am still in the game of life and I am going to win. I have to look at it that way, or I'll just be sad about not playing baseball.

So I'll just keep moving until I get this perfect.

Anyway, back to the analysis.

After my parents feared for my sanity (and fed me), Louie told me that when she started college, she imagined she'd study theater and write plays and perform them for the world. But so did a lot of other people, and she realized they were better than she was, so she started helping them get people to come to their plays by making signs and promoting the plays and that kind of thing. And it turned out that she was really good at that. Better than she was at writing plays.

"Life surprises you," she said. "The lessons you learn the best aren't always the ones you start out looking for."

I really don't know what lesson I'm supposed to learn, though. I mean, before Piper Bell, no one was really better than me at baseball. At Luther, I had my win streak and life was perfect, so deep down, I feel like I know all the lessons, and there is just something about Piper Bell that has made my life go haywire.

So I took Louie's story to mean that maybe it will turn out that field hockey is my sport, and my destiny is to be a better field hockey player than I ever even was a baseball player.

Seeing as I'd always been a **GREAT** baseball player, that could only mean I would be **FIELD HOCKEY CHAMPION OF THE WORLD**.

All night, I dreamt of my victories and imagined how I'd tell this story years from now as I led my future field hockey team to Olympic gold. When I woke up, my neck was sore from all the medals I had to wear in my dreams.

As the day wore on, I kept reminding myself of the dream because I wasn't totally psyched about field hockey yet.

I even took the long route to our bus for my first field hockey game, just so I could look at the baseball team. I didn't want them to see me or anything, so I stayed a good distance from the fence. I was hoping that it wouldn't bother me to see the baseball field, but instead the pit of my stomach ached and I just wanted to run out there and say, "Take me back!" But I couldn't. The team sure didn't seem to miss me. And they looked good, like the kind of team that had gotten rid of its jinx. I watched Devon throw a superfast pitch into Ryder's glove like she was some kind of superstar. I watched Mario crack a hit far into center field. I watched Madeleine make a perfect catch, with no injuries to her nose.

They looked like winners. And they would be, especially without a jinx like me to hold them back.

Bob: *Is this a low point for Gabby? I think so.*
Judy: *She doesn't want to admit it, but she's fearing the worst.*

I wished they'd shut up. I could feel my whole body wanting to be out there with the team, but I had to keep going. Field hockey. I was a field hockey player, about to play her first game, even though I'd never practiced the sport before.

But I needed to talk myself into it. There's a famous Shakespeare saying my dad likes to quote whenever he is behind on one of his work deadlines, "All things are ready, if our mind be so."

Not only were my parents full of helpful quotes, but also I figured I could make my mind ready.

So, with my uniform on and a loaner stick (until I could get my own), plus being all studied up on field hockey and even our opponents (they had an okay record but nothing great), I told myself to be ready.

I told myself to be better than ready. I knew I could score on this opponent.

A goal in my first game? Yup, I was planning on it.

But I was nervous when I met the team at the bus turnaround.

AND THEN THERE WERE HUGS.

"Hey, Gabby," said Molly Oliver, the eighth-grade captain. "Welcome to Penguin field hockey." And she hugged me.

Then Katy Harris hugged me, too. She sort of sang my name, "Gabby Garcia, you're looking fierce in our colors!" Being hugged by her was like being hugged by a star—not just a star like a celebrity but an actual star from the sky. In a good way, not a pointy-edges, "it burns!" way.

Then I got a hug from Colin Reedy. And a girl named Sophia Rodriguez, who I'd seen doing skateboard tricks on the steps leading up to the school. She gave me a hug and a fist bump and said, "This is gonna be so wicked."

It was kind of wicked to be hugged by so many people. They were really happy about me. Maybe it was just an inner-peace yoga thing but it seemed like a good sign.

Coach Raddock slapped me five and asked if I was looking forward to my first game. I said, "Yes!" with a lot of enthusiasm. And then she said, "I have a good feeling about this."

It was how I wished Coach Hollylighter had acted about me.

So maybe I was on the verge of Golden Child status already.

I was definitely feeling better about being here.

We were all standing around, smiling at each other for so long that it started to get weird. You can't just stand around smiling with people for too long without it getting weird. Just a fact.

But then the bus doors opened with that bus-door-opening noise—not to be gross but it sort of sounds like Dumpster farting—and I sighed in relief. "Game time!" I said, because I really didn't know anyone yet. Except in a hugging way.

"Game time, indeed," said a boy named Arlo Cole, who

looked like he was about my brother Peter's age but sounded like someone in one of Louie's TED Talks videos. "After you. Not because you're female, but because you're new."

Okay, weird, but nice. I plopped into a seat on the bus, hoping that I'd found my place. I definitely had no yips—it would be hard to forget how to play field hockey since I'd never played before. But I didn't feel yippy at all.

I felt more **YIPPEE!**

I was so comfortable that when we pulled away from the school I knelt up on my seat and looked around the bus at my teammates. To no one in particular, but also to everyone, I said, "So, I heard Dorchester's only so-so. What's our strategy today?"

After my baseball team experience, I hoped this wasn't annoying to them, but it seemed like a good question.

Molly smiled. It was a great big smile. I figured she was already grateful to have me on the team.

"Well, we are going to play our best." Her voice sounded like a yoga voice, soft and airy like the foam on one of Louie's lattes.

But her strategy was kind of Sports 101. Playing your best could apply to playing Candy Land.

"So, by 'best,' do we have some key plays you can fill me in on? Like, I've seen some cool moves online. I was thinking that I'm pretty fast, and with my baseball skills, if someone could flick the ball my way, I can deflect it off my stick into the goal."

I really sounded like I knew what I was talking about. I was pretty impressed with my mastery of field hockey lingo.

And everyone was looking at me and listening.

They must have been impressed as well.

"Deflect?" Grace Chang, a girl in my social studies class, said. She snapped her gum and I was somewhat relieved that someone on the team sounded like a twelve-year-old. "Sure, we can try that."

I got the sense she'd never really tried deflecting in field hockey. Unless you counted her deflecting my entire idea for getting a win.

"Yes, we'll do our thing," Molly said, and smiled with confidence. I waited to hear what "our thing" was but she didn't say anything else.

I sat back down and stared at the seat in front of me. At Luther, the bus ride to away games was when all my team-mates and I would get psyched for the coming game, talking about our opponents, singing the school song, getting pumped up to play and to win. The field hockey team seemed to be more preoccupied than psyched. It was a letdown after all the hugs.

Was this part of doing their thing?

My stomach knotted up, wondering if they knew what

their thing was but I didn't. It was going to be like the base-ball team's "rapport" all over again. What good were hugs if you felt cut out of the core plays and strategy?

The hugs were **LIES**.

I popped up in my seat again. Maybe I just needed to try harder.

"So is our strategy more offense-based or defense-strong?"

Molly shrugged and turned around to Katy, who was sitting in the seat behind her and writing something in a notebook. "What do you think, Katy? Are we stronger on offense or defense?"

Now we were talking. Really talking: with Katy and her star power in the mix, it was like a mini-team conference. I was being brought in on the important stuff.

Katy looked up from her writing and laughed. "Well, we're strong, for sure. But offense or defense? Gabby, girl, maybe we're good at a little of both." Okay, she sounded like a baby Beyoncé. I thought she was far and away the coolest person I'd ever met in my life and even though what she'd told me made no sense, I was willing to accept it.

Almost.

"But, I mean, do you have anything you want me to do?"

Katy beamed at me. It was mysterious and also frustrating. "Gabby, sweetie, you'll see."

You'll see? Those didn't seem like the words of encouragement you want to share with the player who could help you start to win some games.

I sank into my seat, believing that the team had some kind of team-only telepathy where they were all communicating with brain waves and my brain waves were just sitting there, riding the bus.

See, yet another time when telepathy would have come in handy. Note to self: work on ESP skills.

As Katy went back to writing in her notebook—I tried to see it; was it a play??? But no, it appeared to be music and lyrics for something titled "See the Day"—I told myself to be patient. I wasn't always good at that. But maybe I'd see.

So I turned to my playbook, where I'm writing all this down. It gives me something to do besides worry. I mean, the stakes aren't that high. I even told Dad and Louie not to come to any games until I get into the groove. After all their questions, it seemed like the safest way to handle things for now.

We're pulling up to Dorchester, a school that looks a lot like Piper Bell, with fancy bricks and trees and everything. Okay, taking a deep, yoga-like breath. Not knowing is okay. Even without a goal and a strategy, I have a team and I have me.

And that baseball-field-green grass I love so much?

The field hockey pitch, I can see from my window, is the same beautiful color.

It charges me up instantly.

I'm making my mind ready. This is going to be the best first game of field hockey a person has ever played.

That win streak is on its way!

REPLAY: THE GAME

Win streak . . . nope.

That first Piper Bell baseball game only *seemed* like the **WORST GAME OF MY LIFE**.

Because fifteen minutes into the first half, it's clear: my first field hockey game is **THE WORST GAME OF MY LIFE**.

But this time, it's not due to me.

THIS TEAM IS BAD.

THEY ARE SO.

SO.

BAD.

"Great work out there, Garcia," Coach Raddock says, and I chug a paper cup of water to avoid her eyes. I wish the time-out could last forever. "Keep it up."

Keep what up? I'm scribbling this down just so I can

remind myself: I'm playing my heart out. And, even in my first game, I'm actually pretty good. Not as good as I am at baseball, but I'm naturally athletic and I'm handling the ball well and have pretty good stick control.

Ugh, gotta go back . . .

Back on the bus now. It only got worse after that last update, Here's the full recap. The "do our thing" thing Molly had mentioned? Well, one thing's clear about that thing.

THIS TEAM HAS NO IDEA WHAT ITS THING IS.

Whatever we'd done seemed to be the exact opposite of what the Dorchester Demons had done. By the end of the first half, they were easily beating us, 3–0.

And none of my fellow Penguins seemed upset about this at all.

Katy, who I'd hoped just was cool and mysterious with her "you'll see" talk, pulled on my sleeve. "Gabby, girl, your energy is killin' it."

I wanted to ask if my energy was killin' it, was her energy already dead? But I didn't.

Colin Reedy did a tap dance with no actual taps on his way back to the field for the second half. "Isn't this a joyful, glorious game?" The statement was, I thought, his version of a joke. Then he smiled at me like he really meant it.

"Yeah, definitely," I lied, wondering if he'd been playing the same game I had. The same awful, not glorious, game.

But the whole team was like Colin, smiling and happy, like we weren't getting crushed by our opponent.

How could anyone be having FUN in this game? I wondered. I wanted to **WIN**. I wanted, at least, to look like a team that knew what winning **WAS**.

Maybe it was a strategy, I thought, as Dorchester put the ball into play. Maybe we were about to come on strong. I know Johnny had said the team wasn't very good, but he would have told me if he knew they were this bad, right?

At the start of the second half, the Dorchester Demons had the ball, so we were on defense. Diego's info was solid: there was a ton of running in this game, and I had sort of defaulted to a midfielder spot, which meant I covered almost the whole pitch, heading toward our goal when we were in possession and then doubling back to the Dorchester goal when we were defending against them scoring.

The Demons forward-flicked the ball toward our goal and I made a break in the same direction as the ball. Molly was our goalkeeper.

On a positive note, Molly was energetic. She bounced from foot to foot, swayed from side to side, and hopped onto her toes, like someone who wanted to be ready to block anything.

The only problem was, she blocked **NOTHING**. On the Demons' first three points, it almost seemed like she invited the ball into the goal. Like with a red carpet and some pre-party snacks. She may have even asked it how it was doing and if it had a nice weekend.

So I came up with a strategy: if I played the whole field, maybe I could stop Dorchester from scoring yet again. I noticed that several of my teammates were running up alongside me, but I got the sense it was more to follow me than to follow the ball.

I tried not to let them distract me and closed in on the Demon midfielder who was dribbling the ball toward their goal. When she let the ball roll a sliver out of her stick's reach—I lunged in and pulled it away.

I turned on my heels and kept the ball close to my stick. I dribbled it in the direction of **OUR** goal as best I could. I was still learning how to do this—my stick caught in the grass here and there, and it was harder to keep track of a moving ball than I'd thought, especially on grass. I'd played street hockey in the cul-de-sac before, but that's pushing a flat puck down the street. Big difference.

With the ball in my possession, I spotted Katy standing just outside the striking circle, so I yelled, "Katy, heads up!"

And I sent the ball in a perfect pass right to her. It might as well have been on a path to kiss Katy's hockey stick right on the mouth (if hockey sticks had mouths).

But Katy **MOVED**! Like she was trying to stay out of the ball's way!

I don't think she meant to, because once she saw the ball roll past her, she scrambled toward it, but a Demon defender already had it and headed back toward their goal.

So I was running **AGAIN**. And, if I was being honest, I was trying to run away from the nagging question I had: had anyone on my team ever played field hockey before?

If I learned the answer was in fact no, that those 35 or so minutes of that exact game were the only ones any of my teammates had ever played, I would not have been surprised.

For a moment, I caught myself fearing the worst: **WAS I A JINX HERE, TOO?**

No, that wasn't it. Because I could have been ready to score a goal from inside the striking circle and Grace Chang would have fallen in front of the ball so that I couldn't.

Or I could have gift-wrapped the ball and presented it to Colin Reedy and he would have returned it . . . to the wrong store.

I could have flown a helicopter over the field and shone a spotlight on the ball that only our captain—our captain!—Molly Oliver could see, with big lights saying, **"DON'T LET THIS GO IN THE GOAL!!"** and she would somehow have made sure the ball got into the goal.

They weren't just bad at field hockey. They might have been allergic to it.

But after every play (if you could call them plays), they were so happy.

I ran, I zigged, I zagged, I flicked the ball, I dribbled it.

Sometimes I would hit the ball to another player and get hopeful. On one of these passes, Arlo got a good piece of the ball. He gave it a good whack, but ended up sending it completely out of bounds.

Wait, am I being negative? Maybe I'm overlooking highlights.

(LONG PAUSE WHILE I TRY TO THINK OF HIGHLIGHTS)

HIGHLIGHT REEL

• There was one highlight. *One.*

At the start of the second half, I made it all the way down the field and into the striking circle and I scored a goal. This should be more exciting. However:

I am worried I sort of stole the ball from my own teammate. Sophia had the ball, she was kind of dribbling it but then the ball sort of got away from her and rolled toward me. She was running for it like she meant to keep hitting it but I sort of pretended it was a pass to me and took control of the ball.

The whole trip down the field, I felt bad about the possibility of having stolen it from her.

...DID I STEAL THIS BALL?

When I finally got the ball to the striking circle and flicked it toward the goal, I swear the Dorchester goalie moved ever so slightly to the side to let the ball go in. She definitely didn't reach out to block it. She might have smiled at me. I think she felt sorry for me.

We ended the game losing to Dorchester 7–1. So I got my goal. But it was a **PITY GOAL**.

WINS: 3
LOSSES: 8

STEALING SECOND

Goal: Find out if the game was a one-off bad game or if the team always plays like that.
Action: Slyly "steal" information the way you steal a base—you don't just go for it out in the open, but you sneak toward it.

Post-Day Analysis,
April 30, Part Two

Okay, after writing up the game on the bus, I think I figured some things out.

I was confused because everyone was talking happily. After a huge loss.

It wasn't that I thought we'd win or anything, but I didn't think we'd lose so badly. I didn't even think it was possible to lose so badly. I started to think maybe it wasn't. Maybe it was a fluke. Maybe I could figure it out, without coming right out and asking, "Are you always **THIS BAD**?"

That's what a stinky base stealer does—they stare at second base like it's their birthday and the base is a cake with candles, like it's all theirs for the taking.

And then the second baseman can pour on the defense because the runner isn't even trying to hide anything.

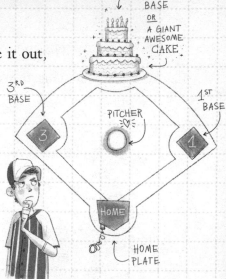

Plus, a good pitcher—like me—will keep them away from that cake at all costs.

So I knew asking right out was a sure way to get the team's defenses all up.

Good base stealers always seem to be looking somewhere else when they make their move.

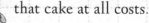

ME GUARDING ~~THE CAKE~~ 2ND BASE!

The best base stealers I've encountered must have eyes on the side of their head because you never know they're even thinking about making a move.

Then, *poof*! They'll be on base and looking like they just got to eat all the icing flowers off the cake before anyone could have one.

AND SECONDS LATER.....

Also, conversationally, I had to seem like I didn't really care about the information I **REALLY, TRULY CARED ABOUT**.

Trying to hide the disappointment on my face, I leaned over my seat to talk to Molly Oliver and said, "So that game was . . . ," and trailed off. I couldn't just blurt out: "That game was a **NIGHTMARE WRAPPED IN AN APOCALYPSE FILLED WITH STINKY CHEESE AND ENCASED IN PEPPERMINT**." (Note to Old Me in case Old Me likes stinky cheese and peppermint: current me hates peppermint, and pair it with stinky cheese? Gross.)

"You were great!" she said, and the way she gave me a captain-like high five, it was hard not to feel really happy about the way I played. I **WAS** good. Maybe the team had just had an off day. Maybe Molly was trying to say that I'd been a great highlight in a game of lowlights.

But then she added, for everyone to hear, "It was such a great game, **TEAM**! I'm so proud of our winning spirit! We are the protagonists in our journeys, never forget!"

But we'd **LOST**. I sensed she wasn't paying a lot of attention, to me or to the team. Because our journey had led us to a stinky, stinky game. But everyone started talking about game moments like they were good moments.

"When you almost blocked that goal, Molly, that was super!"

"Colin, your footwork was amazing right before that Demons defender got the ball from you."

"Which time?"

"All of them!"

Katy Harris was singing. Yes, *singing*. A happy tune. It must have been one of her originals because it wasn't a song I'd heard before. "We got the touch! We got the way! We got the spirit and the sway! We got this! We got that! Take a note, write it down, and **STAT**!"

It was very confusing. They were so . . . positive.

I'd lost games before, and while I **HATE** losing, it wasn't the end of the world or anything. But I was never so weirdly **HAPPY** about it.

Maybe they didn't understand what happened.

I must have looked like I'd seen a ghost, because Coach Raddock stepped up beside my seat.

"Are you okay?" she asked. "How'd you feel about your first game? You looked good!"

"Thanks," I said, looking around. "So, that game was . . . good?"

She nodded. "Yeah, better than usual, in fact."

WHA—??? I took a deep breath and exhaled. I needed to start doing yoga if I wasn't going to explode into a million pieces from all this losing.

"You look confused," Coach Raddock said. "I think we didn't really explain the team to you because, well, time was short and you really seemed interested in the field hockey part."

When she said that, I thought of the baseball team. And how I'd spied on them before the game. Longingly spied on them, to be exact.

"The thing about the team is, they're all really good at something else," she said. "It's been that way for a long time. Piper Bell, who founded the school, was good at a lot of things. She was one of the first women to run a successful peach orchard. She could fly planes. She helped build one of the area's first libraries. And when she started the school, she had this vision of creating Renaissance Students—people who were gifted in a lot of arenas."

"But they're **NOT** . . . ," I started to say, "gifted in this arena" but I knew those were the wrong words.

"Piper Bell started the field hockey team for her favorites," Coach Raddock said, getting a misty-eyed, admiring look.

"They were all really great students and also talented in at least one other area. So the tradition became that the field hockey team was not that good because it brought together the students who were destined for greatness in these other areas."

YES, SHE SAID BEING BAD WAS A FIELD HOCKEY TRADITION.

I imagined decades of Piper Bell field hockey players, all tripping and falling and missing the ball and hitting each other in the shins with sticks and big, lit-up zeros on scoreboard after scoreboard.

That couldn't be true!

A TRADITION OF AWFULNESS

"Say that again—a tradition of being **BAD** at field hockey?"

"More or less, yes," Coach Raddock said. "But it's not like we're not winners.

"Team," Coach said. "I think we need to bring Gabby in on our true goal."

She said it just like that. It was like being in a movie where the lead character has been surrounded by mysterious circumstances and then suddenly a secret door opens and she only has to pass through it for everything to be explained.

"Oh, you want the full story," Molly said, like she'd been waiting her whole life to tell it. "I love telling the full story. I'm a writer, you know."

And even though she was a terrible goalie, when she said she was a writer, something told me she's much better at that than at goalkeeping.

She explained that everyone on the team had a story. Or, really, a "something," as she put it.

"What I mean is, everyone has a passion that's not field hockey. But the philosophy we have is, if we allow ourselves to just be bad or at least *unconcerned* with field hockey, it gets the ya-yas out for our other thing. So, because I might mess up at a game, where it doesn't matter, I am able to write better because I feel like I left all my screwups out there on the pitch," Molly said.

"The ya-yas?" I asked.

"Yes, ya-yas. They're internalizations that make you think you don't know what you're doing," she said. She had a much better vocabulary than she did reflexes.

"Like a bunch of little yous running around in your head saying you're bad at something or can't do it?" It sounded like the yips.

"Wow, that's a great way to put it, yes!" She nodded and even wrote it down.

She gave me the lowdown on her true, winner talent.

MOLLY OLIVER

MOLLY OLIVER

(a.k.a. GIANT OF WORDS)

Height: Very tall, but a giant of words
Build: An amazon of creative power
Role model: The Brontë Sisters with a side of J. K. Rowling
Special skills: Marathon reading, able to write whole chapters in a single bound, can quote Jane Austen effortlessly
Quote: "Writers live twice." —Natalie Goldberg

Katy Harris, the co-captain, went next. I was not surprised when she told me she was born to be a star. She had that power.

KATY HARRIS

(a.k.a. BABY BEYONCÉ)

Height: Three-quarters of a Beyoncé—a baby Beyoncé
Build: Singing-dancing double threat
Role Model: Beyoncé
Special Skills: Catchy lyric writing, on-the-fly choreography creation
Quote: "If everything was perfect, you would never learn and you would never grow." —Beyoncé

Katy and Molly introduced everyone else. Colin Reedy: tap dancer. Sophie Rodriguez: star skateboarder with a specialty in heart-stopping stunts. Marilyn Hu: the next Marie Curie. Arlo Cole: a preteen diplomat with a talent for debate. Dominic Alimento: an amazing photographer, and with a real camera, not a phone! Lisa Clover: an "illusionist"—she doesn't like being called a magician—who can make a rabbit float. Arnold Kapoor: the greatest actor of his very-young generation. Grace Chang: an ambidextrous street artist (which means she can control two spray paint cans at once).

My mind, just like the character in the movie who learns all this stuff at once, was blown. "But we haven't told you the best part," Katy Harris said, and she stood up on her seat, which couldn't have been very safe. "We're a squad with a mission. So, get this, we aren't just doing these things for ourselves. Don't get me wrong, that's all enlightened and stuff. But we're kind of . . . champions."

Winners. Champions. They were all speaking my language. "How?"

Katy smiled. "The United States Preteen Talent Showcase." She said it like I knew what it was.

I didn't.

"What's that?"

"Our ticket to fame," Katy said, and the competitive glint in her eye was inspiring. "As long as we win."

The talent showcase, she explained, was a regional competition in the Atlanta area and featuring the multitalented student teams from the top area middle schools. The show would be broadcast on the internet in less than a month, and people from the Atlanta region would vote on the best school talent team. The talents could be a range of things. Competitors just had to be from the same school.

"The winners go to New York to perform for the national prize, and get to be on TV," Katy said. "And, honestly, not that I'm in it just for me, but once I'm on TV, my act is going to blow up."

She sounded like she had a bit of an ego. She sounded like me, so maybe I did have an ego. At least a small one. But I liked seeing Katy's. And the rest of the team nodded in agreement, so she must have been good.

"Really, we're all worth watching," Katy said. "I don't think there's a chance we can't win. I mean, I don't think losing is an option."

Suddenly, the reason I was on the team was clear. I wasn't going to play field hockey. I wasn't going to play baseball. But I was going to win a competition and be on a national television show.

Being on TV would definitely reboot my win streak. (What can I say? Being a TV star is a big deal and I'm the product of my generation.)

"I mean, but it's cool that you're into field hockey for real," Sophia said. But I didn't feel like that would be cool enough. I wanted a talent. I wanted to compete.

I wanted to fit in with this random team and win the talent showcase.

I've almost never been random. But I thought of Diego, who is always trying to find a sport where he'll be good, or trying new things, and whenever I say, "Hmm, maybe that's not a good idea," he'll get all puffed up and say, "Progress always involves risks. You can't steal second base and keep your foot on first."

He has no idea who said that, except that it wasn't even a baseball player, but for a not-baseball player, it makes a lot of sense.

So before I opened my mouth to agree with Sophia, my brain rushed through possibilities:

I could be a classical painter, maybe? (Because Grace Chang had the market cornered on the street art stuff.)

GABBY GARCIA, PEACH TREE'S OWN PICASSO

Requires: I'd need one of those palette things, a beret, and the ability to say things like, "If you don't understand it, you're not looking hard enough."

Problem: I once tried to paint by numbers and it didn't add up.

Or maybe I could be a fashion designer?

GABBY GARCIA, STYLISTA SUPERSTAR

Requires: Sketchbook, pencils, big sunglasses, a tall model to be my inspiration and living man-nequin, a style idea so amazing that the whole school wants to wear a Gabby original.

Problem: When someone says some-thing about their "look," I think they're talking about checking to see if a runner is stealing second.

Maybe I need to be something more brainy.

Oh, an astronomer, that could work!

GABBY GARCIA, THE GALACTIC GENIUS

Requires: Telescope.

Problem: Planet discovery seems daunting. Plus, look at poor Pluto. It was a planet and they took it away. Maybe a magician?

THE GREAT GABBY

Requires: Top hat, cape, wand, many hours, and a special bond with a rabbit that will disappear and reappear as needed.

Problem: All of the above, as I had a pet rabbit once and it ran away and never came back. Except the top hat, as it would make me look taller. And, darn it, I just remembered that Lisa Clover is a magician. And she can make things float. Me and my nonexistent rabbit won't stand a chance.

A sculptor, that's unusual!

GABBY GARCIA, SHAPER OF DREAMS

Requires: A lot of clay, patience, perseverance, and the ability to see with my hands.

Problem: If my past experience with Play-Doh is any indication, everything I make will resemble a baseball or a worm. It's really hard to make things out of clay!

I stalled out. I had nothing.

Nothing.

Maybe I could have pretended nothing was my talent. I have an older cousin, Jacob, who's studying philosophy, and sometimes he sits in the corner at family parties, and if you ask him what he's thinking about, he'll say, "Nothing," and then will pause and say, "So, really, everything . . . ," in a very dramatic way.

But honestly, Jacob can be really annoying. And philosophy and nothingness are probably a little out there for most middle schoolers. Plus, not very TV-friendly.

I must have been thinking so long that everyone started going back to talking about their talents. Forgetting me entirely. I wanted something to contribute. Especially when I heard them talk. They sounded like **WINNERS**.

"I had the best breakthrough in study hall," Molly said. "The plot twist is that there is no twist! It's *so* not what anyone is expecting!"

"Dope, chica, I can't wait to read it," Sophia said. "Is your main character's best friend still a skateboarder?"

"Yes—thanks for letting me shadow you," Molly said. "I'm going to list you in the acknowledgments."

"This weekend, I'm auditioning backup dancers, because honestly my last ones were **BLAH**," Katy said, popping into the conversation. "If y'all know anyone, I'll give you the details."

"Sure thing," Grace said. "My older sister's dance team would love to work with you. Did I ever tell you they taught themselves the moves from your last video?"

My teammates were writing books! And songs! And making up dance moves! Sophia was so good at skateboarding that she was an expert for Molly Oliver, who, yes, **WROTE A BOOK**!!

What had I been doing with my life?

I opened my mouth a few times to talk but nothing came out. I was just going to be an ex-baseball player playing field hockey on a bad field hockey team full of amazing people.

I was all washed up and only twelve years old.

"Oh, but don't say too much about the actual video part," Katy reminded everyone. "When this thing drops, it's going to bust up YouTube."

"I won't say a word about what I just heard," I said. Because I wouldn't. Because I had contributed nothing to society. Life was meaningless. I should talk to Jacob.

"Ha! Word! Heard! You rhymed!" Molly looked excited. "You're a poet and we didn't know it!"

Poet?

POET!

Requires: Pencil, paper, rhyming words.

Problems: None! I'd just rhymed without even thinking about it, didn't I? I was a **POET!!** Who knew??

Suddenly, I was not Gabby Garcia, inconsequential middle schooler.

I was Gabby Garcia, poet, and it would only be a matter of time before I was reading one of my works to a crowd of stunned and inspired fans, who couldn't believe that such beautiful words came from the pen of someone so young.

Stunned and inspired fans watching me on **TELEVISION**.

I shrugged, trying not to let on that I was extremely excited to have accidentally landed on my "thing."

"I dabble," I said. I already sounded like a poet—a little mysterious and modest. Was that what poets sounded like?

"That's so cool!" Katy said. "Who's your favorite poet?"

Oh no. Could I say Dr. Seuss?

No, poets were mysterious. Carefully, I said, "Well, you know . . ."

"Katy!" Molly said. "You can't ask her to pick just one! I mean, there's Yeats and Keats and Whitman and Plath and Rossetti and Collins and Dickinson. Right, Gabby? I mean, let's not forget Cummings and Langston Hughes and—really, Katy, trust me when I say Gabby doesn't have one favorite."

I nodded like Molly had just said the most important thing in the world. And she did, in a way. Who knew there were that many poets??? I was just relieved she answered the question for me.

"I can't believe I didn't know there was another writer in our midst!" Molly's eyes were glimmering excitedly. "So, do you write, like, at home or do you go to a coffeehouse or something?"

Coffee? Yuck. I really hoped I don't have to start drinking coffee to be a convincing poet.

"Usually at home," I said. "I like my privacy. It's very crucial to my process." I think my dad said that to me and my brother once when he was behind on a deadline and Louie laughed at him because, up until that point, my dad had wandered into the living room about 400 times "just to see what everyone else was doing."

But no one laughed at me. Actually, Sophia nodded like this made perfect sense. "The rhymes probably flow better that way," she said.

Katy shook her head. "Girl, poems don't have to rhyme! Gabby'll tell you. There's freestyle. Isn't that right, Gabby?"

I actually didn't know this. I glanced sideways at Molly, looking for some kind of nod that this was true but she was furiously writing notes into a journal. So, since Katy seemed sure about it, I said, "Yup, poems have to be whatever they want to be."

Now Lisa, the magician (who I swear hadn't been any-where near us two seconds ago, that's how good she is at magic!), said, "That's really, really poetic." (Side note: this was the first time I'd ever heard her talk. I was pretty sure most of the team didn't hear her voice that often.)

Molly tilted her head to the side and looked at me as if she was deciding something very important. Then she said, "You know, I didn't know there was so much to you, Gabby. Guys, don't you think she should join us as part of the showcase?"

Katy rolled her eyes. "Of course Gabby should. We don't have a poet yet!" Then she looked at me and grinned. "But, yeah, you need to hang out with all of us. We'd love it."

As the rest of the team nodded and got excited about me joining them for this hangout, I felt my new poet self begin-ning to take over. And as I write this now, in the privacy of my room, I've decided, yes, I'm going to be a poet. No, actu-ally, I **AM** a poet.

I grinned and inspiration struck:

"You don't have to ask me twice. That would be super-nice!"

A WIN! I'M IN!

WINS: 4
LOSSES: 8 (but on the verge of a major turnaround!)

THE POET AND
YOU DIDN'T KNOW IT

Goal: Alongside my new team, win the United States Preteen
Talent Showcase.
Action: Be a poet? (There is no rulebook for this!)

Post-Day Analysis:
May 1

With my new true goal in mind, I suddenly felt better. Poetry
was easy, right?

I went to bed last night thinking so, and woke up charged
to write something.

But, then . . . .

Winning, a Poem by Gabby Garcia

I like more than anything to win
It's always just been who I am
With winning in mind, is how I begin
My poetic quest to (PUT RHYME HERE)
Some people say to win is not the only thing
Those people are wrong
Sorry if you don't agree,
The thrill of victory is the best
Losing is the worst
I can't think of the rest
Poetry is hard.

Okay, very hard.

The good thing was that I finally felt positive about my direction. I knew where my win would come from: the talent showcase, which my team—no, talent squad—felt confident we could win. And in this case, I wouldn't have to prove myself with rapport or be the jinx or be the one doing all the work on the field. They had a lot of talent, so now I just needed to develop mine.

But I also had a lot of catching up to do at school. I still had that C in history. And my grades in English and algebra were veering toward B territory.

The guidance counselor wanted to meet with me because my grades had dropped from Luther and she wanted to know how I was "adjusting." That word again. I went to see her and it was awkward. I was trying to make it quick because I had a poetry career to start.

Me: Hi, Ms. Counselor. It's nice of you to be concerned but I'm fine!

Guidance Counselor: Ms. Garcia, you don't need to be ashamed if this is a hard transition for you. You've been through a lot.

Me: But I think I've figured things out. I feel great, honest!

Guidance Counselor: May I at least give you some pamphlets to help you? And maybe you can visit again when you're ready to discuss your situation?

Me: Do you have any pamphlets on how to write poetry?

Guidance Counselor (with concerned face): What are you trying to express, Ms. Garcia? Do you have some feelings you'd like to explore?

Me: What feelings do you think you'd vote for, if I wrote about them?

Guidance Counselor: I'm confused.

Me: Hmm. It seems like you need some time to think about that. Gotta go!

And then Johnny made a comment in algebra that bugged me.

"So how's field hockey?" he asked.

"Great! Marvelous! Stupendous!" I was tapping into my entire vocabulary so my poems might be better. "Did you know about all their talents? I'm going to be the team poet."

He frowned. "Yeah, I know about them; it's school tradition. But, poetry, you just decided that?" He looked down at his notebook of numbers like there'd be some explanation there. "Don't you feel weird to not play baseball? I, um, took a look at your old stats. You were a really good pitcher at Luther. And now you're just . . . quitting?"

I said, in a hushed whisper, "You're the one who said they needed one good player. And you never mentioned the talent stuff."

Johnny's eyes went wide. "I **DID** say that, but it was just a hypothetical. I didn't think someone who loved baseball the way you seem to, and who can play like you can, would actually quit to join **FIELD HOCKEY**."

Oh. I didn't know what to say to that. Thank goodness Mr. Patler handed out a pop quiz so I didn't have to think about it. Johnny was right. I wasn't totally comfortable quitting the sport I'd played my whole life. Not at all. But I hadn't been comfortable since I got here. And now I felt, well, pretty okay. I did quit the Penguins, but I'd had my reasons. The talent showcase was something I could win this year, and next year I'd be back at Luther and everything would go back to normal. Normal, with me playing baseball and being the Golden Child again and not being called a jinx. Why couldn't he mind his own business? And also, be more specific and not **HYPOTHETICAL**!

Besides, there were already plenty of non-hypothetical positives. At lunch, the field hockey team—um, talent showcase squad?—had called me over to sit with them.

(I'm still running the Scope, Ditch, and Switch every morning, though. Today, Dad had packed me some kind of double-decker sandwich made from assorted leftovers that might have been okay to eat but even in my lunch pack was leaning to one side like a condemned skyscraper. Oh, that's a simile!)

Now that I had a team that wanted me on it, Piper Bell was starting to feel like my school instead of some place I got left because no one else wanted me. I was definitely not a Luther Polluter anymore. The only thing is, until I really get the hang of poetry, I'm still a little lost talking to the talent squad. I don't exactly have a ton of works in progress to discuss.

So I decided to keep being mysterious. It was working pretty well. Like this scene from lunch, which we ate in an empty classroom. Molly called it an Inspiration Meet-Up:

I knew with the right motivation I'd be fine. I just needed a cheerleader to get me on the right path, to tell me to get in the game and write poetry. So I went to my number one fan, Diego. He was at the wonky internet café and the connection for our video call was so bad we had to use an ancient form of communication: instant messaging. It wasn't very instant, at all. I'm shocked our parents have made it as far as they have.

Diego260: How was the field hockey game?

Gabbyrulez: Awful! So awful!!

Diego260: Ugh. I'm sorry. Did you not like it? How was the team?

Gabbyrulez: The team might be the worst field hockey players alive.

Diego260: Hmm. Maybe you can get back on the baseball team?

Gabbyrulez: Nope. To them I'm a jinx, remember?

Diego260: I think you're giving up too easy on them. Why would you want to be on a bad field hockey team when you can be on a good baseball team? You love baseball!

Gabbyrulez: But the field hockey team is actually a TALENT SQUAD. And with our combined talents, we're going to win a trip to New York to be on NATIONAL TV.

Diego260: So is your talent baseball?

Gabbyrulez: No. Not to them. I'm a poet.

Diego260: Wait . . . What? Huh?

Gabbyrulez: Yup. Poetry. Cool, right?

Diego260: You've never written a poem in your life.

Gabbyrulez: No. But I will. And I sort of did. It's just a bad poem.

Diego260: Gabby, I don't mean to sound unsupportive, but this sounds bad.

Gabbyrulez: . . .

Diego260: Don't be mad. But, poetry?

Gabbyrulez: I'm sure there's been a poetic baseball player. One, two, three, tell me!

Diego260: Uh, I guess Yogi Berra said some poetic things. But he never quit baseball.

Gabbyrulez: I'm not quitting. It's a hiatus. When there's no more asbestos at Luther, I'm back.

Diego260: I'll send you some Yogi Berra thoughts. But I still think this is weird.

Gabbyrulez: So is living among the monkeys of Costa Rica.

Diego260: That's not my fault!! My parents feed me and I'm a growing boy. I have to go where they go.

Gabbyrulez: You're tall enough.

Diego260: Be nice, or I won't send you those Yogi-isms.

Gabbyrulez: You're the best, Diego.

And he was the best, but I really needed some poetic insight. I needed an expert opinion. Expert meaning "old person."

My dad was in the kitchen, with his hands literally in the butt of a chicken. Maybe asking him for advice was a horrible idea.

WOULD YOU ASK FOR ADVICE FROM THIS MAN?

It was a dead chicken, a grocery store chicken, not one with feathers. But still, it seemed like he was having some trouble with it because the whole bird kept sliding off his hands into the pan. It didn't help that he kept looking away from his project to check the score on the baseball game playing on the living room TV.

"Hey, Gabby, just doing a spice rub on this bird. I'm try-ing something new: an *interior* spice rub. Flavor inside and out." He grinned and dipped his fingers in a bowl of spices, then massaged the top of the chicken very lovingly. I won-dered if I should play some romantic music for them.

"Maybe I should let you get back to work . . . ," I said, backing out of the kitchen.

"Nah, what do you need?" Dad washed his hands at the

sink and wiped them on his apron, which has a picture of a pig and Cupid on it and says, "Love at First Bite." The chicken was probably jealous.

"Just, well, how do you become a poet?" I asked.

He leaned against the counter and looked thoughtfully around the kitchen. "A poet? I guess you write some poems."

"Dad! That's not helpful!"

"Well, most hard questions have simple answers that are hard to hear," he said.

"Yeah," Peter piped up from the kitchen counter, where he was supposed to be doing his homework but was actually drawing a large, drooling swamp monster. "Like when Gabby annoys me, I should simply make her go away but it's not that easy. The truth hurts. Me most of all."

"I'll show you a truth that hurts," I threw back, not knowing how I'd actually do this.

My dad held up his hands and said, "Stop! I wanna hear the game." Hearing sports goings-on is a go-to peacekeeping measure in our house.

Peter stuck out his tongue out at me and went back to drawing. My dad and I both paused to watch Andre Ethier's at bat against the Braves. Our pitcher walked him. We shrugged at each other. It could have been worse.

"So . . . poetry . . . ," I said, rubbing my hands together. "What can you tell me?"

I was expecting something good. My dad was a writer, after all.

But then he shrugged. "It's not like baseball, Gabs," he said.

Not to be disrespectful, but that was a big "no duh."

But he went on. "I mean, baseball is very ordered and structured in a way. There are rules and a way of playing, so even when a game has surprises, they still fit into something bigger," he said. "Poetry has some structure, sometimes, but it's more like a feeling. It doesn't always make sense, until it does."

"Baseball is kind of like a feeling, sometimes," I said, and thought how it had been way too long since I'd been on a ball field, even if it had only been about a week. It really stunk. Even filling my brain with poetic thoughts and appreciation for my new friends couldn't entirely push baseball from my mind. It really was like breathing to me.

Dad examined his chicken, rubbing more spices here and there like it was a baby who needed rash cream. "Hmm, you're right," he said. "Maybe you're more of a poet than me."

"Who's a poet?" Louie said, coming in the back door and tossing her workbag on the table. She gave Dad a kiss on the cheek and raised an eyebrow at the chicken.

Dad looked from her to me. "I don't know . . . Gabby, why the sudden interest in poetry?"

I'd already told them to give me time to get used to field hockey before they saw me play. And that was more so *they* could get used to it. I didn't want to give them another **NEW GABBY** thing. I'd have to eat the whole chicken to prove I was feeling okay. Better to just become an amazing poet, win the talent show, and then reveal my new plan. Once it had all worked out for me.

"School project," I said, because that would put an end to all further questions.

Except mine.

Was this a win? A loss? The start of a poem?

WINS: 4
LOSSES: 8 (holding steady while things are too close to call)

POETIC-ISH THINGS YOGI BERRA SAID, ACCORDING TO DIEGO

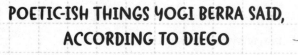

• "When you come to a fork in the road, take it."

• "You can observe a lot just by watching."

• "The future ain't what it used to be."

• "It gets late early out there."

- "If the world were perfect, it wouldn't be."

- "No one goes there nowadays, it's too crowded."

- "It ain't over till it's over."

ODE TO A SPICY CHICKEN
By Gabby Garcia

Oh, chicken, oh, chicken,

Fresh from the store,

I wonder if you knew

What you were in for

When you landed in our kitchen.

Oh, chicken, oh, chicken,

Did you have any clue

What would happen to you?

Forgive my father.

He is very enthusiastic.

If you were still alive,

You would sneeze.

Do chickens sneeze?

Is this a poem?

POETRY IN MOTION

Goal: Live up to my poetic promise.
Action: Take on a step-by-step plan to be the best poet I can be. (For all the world to see. On TV! Yes. I'm committed to this.)

Post-Day Analysis:
May 5

No one was really going to help me figure out this poetry thing, I could see. The people most likely to be useful—the field hockey team/talent squad—thought I was already a poet (with amazing field hockey skills), so I needed to sort through this thing myself. I'd have to focus on the poems. In baseball, or any sport really, players can break it down into parts they need to address. Offense, defense, form, speed, agility.

I needed to look at poetry as parts I could put together in the same way.

SO, MY STEP-BY-STEP STRATEGY:

- Read a **LOT** of poetry. (Okay, read **SOME** poetry. It takes a long time when you keep falling asleep, but sometimes poetry is really boring.)

- Dress like a poet. This is harder since poets throughout time have dressed in a lot of ways. But I eliminated ruffled shirts with fancy sleeves (I'm a messy eater and also ruffles seem like a lot of work) and long, flowery dresses. That leaves me with wearing a lot of black— sort of like a uniform—so I'm going with that.

- Have a poetic disposition. I don't know—some of these poets were really depressing. Edgar Allan Poe— that guy was spooky. Emily Dickinson never left her house. Lord Byron was always heartbroken, or, you know, breaking hearts. That's not really my thing. Mysterious but upbeat is going to have to do the trick for me.

- Master a poetic style. Nope, I don't know how I'm going to do this, either. Easy rhymes and free verse are my starting points, but I'm not really getting anywhere, even if I had to start somewhere. (Was that poetic?)

I only had one finished poem so far. The chicken one, I decided, was weird and not finished, but this one was maybe a little better.

It was about clouds because I kept looking out the window while I wrote it (in algebra class, where I'd been avoiding any and all eye contact with Johnny) and clouds seemed more poem-friendly than the value of X.

I ended that last line with no rhyme because **POETIC LICENSE**.

(There's this poet, e. e. cummings, who used all kinds of poetic license. He made up his own words and didn't use capital letters, even in his name. So, if he can do that, I can end my poems however I want. Poetic license would be a fun way to go through life.)

TIMES IT WOULD BE NICE TO SAY "POETIC LICENSE" AND HAVE IT GET YOU OUT OF THINGS

- **Speeding tickets**—"I was driving one hundred in a forty-five because of my poetic license."

Clouds in the sky
~~I~~ don't know why
Sky full of clouds

They are quiet not loud
Sometimes, clouds roll over the
sun
Sometimes a lot, sometimes ~~jus~~ just
one

Clouds in the sky
I don't know why

But there they are.

- **Pop quizzes**—"I answered all the questions with questions because poetic license."

- **Dentist appointments**—"I'm afraid that's not a real cavity and just your imagination. Poetic license."

- **Lackluster report cards**—"I liked the way the Bs and Cs looked together because of poetic license."

- **Trips to weird relatives' houses**—"I have to claim poetic license instead of going to view Uncle Dan's photos of his mushroom-gathering expedition."

I was learning. I could write free verse poems and poems that followed a structure, like limericks or haikus. (Those are both short, too.) And there are poetic devices, like metaphors and similes. We've gone over them in English class. (I need to study up on them because I didn't exactly pay great attention the first time around.)

There is also alliteration, which is when a set of words starts with the same letter or sound. My name, Gabby Garcia, qualifies! In other words, I probably **AM** destined for this poetry thing. Gabby Garcia's got a good grasp of grammar—that's alliteration. (But really, my grammar isn't perfect and that's okay. **POETIC LICENSE!**)

I never think much about words—it's always been my dad's thing—but maybe it's in my bones. Maybe the asbestos at Luther had to happen because I've been a poet all along. Or at least a poet until I win that trophy and the TV showcase.

So as part of my Poet Training Program, I put on my all-black outfit—and a baseball cap, but I called it my thinking cap. I also put on my mitt, because I've missed wearing it. I stared out my window.

More clouds. I'd already written about that.

UGH.

I decided some additional equipment might help, which I'll note here in case future wannabe poets ever seek my advice:

- **Pens**—These would be better if they were the kind with the big feathers coming off the top and the ink that you dip your quill into, but instead I gathered what I could find around the house. Mostly free pens from doctors' offices and real estate agents. But nestled in my drawer was an extra-special set of rainbow-colored gel pens that I'd totally forgotten about. Poets can write in color. They **SHOULD** write in color.

- **Paper**—Obviously. (I could have used a computer but I thought it was more like a poet to scratch things out on paper. It was part of the art form.)

- **A rhyming dictionary**—Who knew there was such a thing? But there is, and my dad has one! It was dusty and made me sneeze so I also needed . . .

- **Tissues**—For the sneezes.

- **A book of Shakespeare's sonnets, for inspiration**—My dad has one of these, too. Also dusty. Need more tissues.

- **Inspiration**—I'd be more inspired by Shakespeare if I understood it all the way, but I was probably not going to learn this till high school. So I needed to make my inspiration. It was a hard thing to get. There wasn't an inspiration aisle at Target. The gel pens helped a little.

After dinner (which was some kind of Thai curry that Peter said was gross but was actually good but would definitely be fed to Dumpster the next morning because Peter is a good barometer of what other kids find gross), I announced to my family that I had to go compose a poem.

"That's so exciting," my dad said. "So you're really into this school project, huh?"

"See, Piper Bell's not so bad," Louie said.

I was wearing a very poet-like black turtleneck—which was kind of hot since it was May in Georgia and I'd just eaten spicy food—but I gave my family my coolest look. **MYSTERY!**

"You're right . . . ," I said, trailing off a bit—**MORE MYSTERY!**—as I took a drink of water. (Note to sweaty self: Rethink poet look. Be the first shorts-wearing poet.) "I wonder if poetry is my new calling." I had to give them some hint so they weren't totally surprised when I showed up on TV winning trophies and trips to New York.

I expected some gasps of astonishment or maybe a "wow" to my admission of my new artistic way of life, but Dad just nodded and looked at Louie.

"She must get that from me," he said. "And my writing."

"You've only written one poem in your life and it had a fart joke in it," Louie told him.

Peter laughed. "Well, Gabby is what would happen if a fart joke wrote a poem. I could write a better poem with my butt."

"Shut up, Peter," I said. But poetically.

"Is that a poem?" he asked.

"You're intruding on my creative energy," I said. Which was a new fancy way to say he was being a total bummer.

I helped myself to a few cookies because I was still waiting for inspiration to strike and I figured a sugar rush was the next best thing. I left for my room, mysteriously. Well, sort of mysteriously, because I had to help clear the table. Then, upstairs, I cleared off some space at my desk and started to write.

Well . . .

Writing might be the wrong word.

It felt like I had hundred-pound weights strapped to each of my fingers.

If I'd had inspiration, I'd know what to write about, but a lot of poems are about true love and stuff and I'm only twelve. (And do **NOT** have a crush on Johnny Madden and even if I did I'm certainly not about to write a poem for him and his questioning-my-every-move ways. If I had a crush, it would be a **HYPOTHETICAL** crush.)

I burped a little Thai-food burp and that made me think about Dumpster. So I started a poem about Dumpster.

DUMPSTER, MY FRIEND

Dogs are man's best friend
They say, to the very end
But what about us girls?
Here's some wisdom, in pearls
At times you have things you don't want to eat
A weird casserole or some odd bits of meat

Well, I know a dog, his name is Dumpster
He'll eat your strange stuff, oh yes he will, sir
He's saved me a bunch of times
From an assortment of lunchbox crimes
I hope one day you meet him, too.
Just bring some food and he'll love you.

I liked the poem and I knew Dumpster would like it, or would eat it, but it didn't exactly feel like prize-winning stuff.

I tried to write one about the monkeys Diego had mentioned in his emails but, well, most of what I knew about them was the poop throwing and that really doesn't seem like something people want to hear about.

I knew I should write about baseball. I had lots of poetic feelings about baseball, love-poem feelings. But if I did that, wouldn't it just prove that I should stop all this poetry stuff and go back to baseball (which I would, eventually, just not now)? I couldn't keep completely overhauling my life, and even if I missed playing baseball, the team I could play for, the Penguins, didn't miss me. So I could write about baseball later, once I'd mastered the art form. Feeling barfy was just part of the process, right?? The creative process. Of not creating . . .

And writing this instead. Because every letter of every word is so hard to think of that it seems like I'm **INVENTING** the alphabet from scratch.

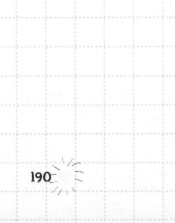

Okay, I stopped for a while to do my algebra homework and it felt so good to just solve problems that had answers that I started to think about changing my talent to math. But, I don't know, I am good at it but not exactly a whiz. And it isn't really something people want to see on TV.

Keep going, Gabby! I'm talking to myself in the pages of my playbook. This may not be a positive development. It's 10:30. I'm so tired . . .

It's 1:47! **A.M.!** Huh?

There's sleep-drool under the neck of my turtleneck. There's no poem on these pages. I'm going to take poetic license and not write and call today a win anyway. Poetic license. 'Cause I'm so tired.

WINS: 5
LOSSES: 8

ALL-TIME GREATS

Shakespeare (William Shakespeare but he's famous enough to go by one name), aka the Bard of Avon

Age: Dead

From: England

Known for: Being a poet, playwright, and some say the greatest writer in the English language

Odd fact: Even though kids like me think of Shakespeare as "fancy," when he was alive, everyone went to see his plays, like they were superhero movies or something.

Cool thing he wrote: "Our doubts are traitors / And make us lose the good we oft might win / By fearing to attempt." (Which means, believe in yourself and try new things! Like being a poet.)

TO BE A BARD—IT'S HARD

Goal: Still to have a worthy finished poem! Come on, inspiration!

Action: I honestly am starting to wonder how I'm going to do this. Seek inspiration, I guess?

Post-Day Analysis:
May 10

Is it just me, or were these plays simpler when I just wanted to get on the baseball team? It's hard to know where to start with some of this stuff. It would have been nice if poetry was for sure in my blood, but who can tell these things? I'm definitely not going to get a poetry blood test. Gross.

I started my official Poet Training Program five days ago and as of this morning was still struggling to finish a poem I felt I could share with the team. But my mysterious thing wasn't going to work forever. While everyone else had their stuff to talk about, I had a big old nothing. When I'd been the Golden Child, I was the reason to talk.

BENEFITS OF BEING THE GOLDEN CHILD

• Solid fan base

• Total confidence

- Awareness you are pretty much perfect

- Winning at life

- Cool nickname

So today, after field hockey practice—well, "practice" because it had mostly been me running up and down the field, passing, dodging, deflecting while most everyone else just bumbled around and Coach Raddock (wrongly) shouted "Great work!" at everyone—I pulled a mysterious-poet move again and said I had to get some air to think about my next poem.

I needed inspiration desperately. Or for a finished poem to fall from the sky. I was starting to get the yips about just existing.

All the talent around me was starting to feel too close for comfort. Instead of being inspired by everyone, I was starting to fear being the weakest link. Or a **JINX**.

Where could I get inspiration? I walked and wondered. And, of course, I found myself at the ball field again, to do a little more staring. With longing. There was a game and a crowd—the Penguins hadn't lost since my jinx day. Devon was on the mound. I could see the cowboy glint in her eye even from far away. (And I stayed far away, tucked behind a cluster of fans standing near the visiting team's bleachers. I was a longing lurker.) Johnny had his head bent over the stats book. I had to make sure he didn't see me or I'd get another speech about how I should have stayed on the team.

Baseball is so nice—three strikes, you're out. Three outs, and the other team comes up. Nine innings, nine players on the field. It has such a great structure. It makes so much sense.

I need poetry to make sense. A blank page is scary.

Maybe that was why Shakespeare liked sonnets.

They have a form and a rhyme scheme and a **STRUCTURE**.

Shakespeare was basically the Babe Ruth of writing and poetry—everything he did was a home run.

Maybe the most baseball kind of poem I could write was a sonnet.

And that was what I was going to do.

An answer! At last.

I tried not to think about how I always seemed to find everything I needed when I was on a baseball field.

It was time to write a sonnet. I had inspiration. Or at least a plan. I'd turned poetry into a play.

WINS: 6
(having a plan is as good as a win at this point!)
LOSSES: 8

THE SONNET IN MY BONNET

Goal: Write a sonnet worthy of the talent showcase.

Action: Write my very first sonnet and have it be good enough to want to read it in front of hundreds of people. Or tens of people. How many people would be watching this thing? Thousands. Had to be.

Post-Day Analysis:
May 13

It would have been really great if sonnets were easier to figure out, like baseball. But after reading a bunch, I just knew they had fourteen lines and a set rhyme scheme. Shakespeare liked to rhyme his in the middle of lines, with something called iambic pentameter, but that was kind of advanced and scared me.

I was going to stick with my version, where the end of each line goes with the rhyme scheme. I'd like to see Shakespeare throw a perfect slider his first time on the mound.

Field hockey practice broke early today, because we have another game tomorrow. We've lost a lot of games. All the games. It isn't even worth thinking about or I get queasy.

I was never going to save this team on the field. I had to count on the talent showcase and things were heating up. It wasn't that far away.

Instead of the pregame yoga session, Coach Raddock said we could take the hour to work on our talent showcase acts. She paired us off with partners. "It's time for some artistic talent exchange, people," she said, sounding way more coach-like than when she was coaching us to play field hockey.

I got paired with Katy. Yup, the most talented of the talent squad, and me. The so-far-unproductive poet. Maybe she'd just want to practice her dance moves and I could get out of having to try to write in front of her.

But she linked arms with me and said, "Let's just sit under

that tree. I write better outside. Don't you?"

"Sure." I nodded. I didn't write better anywhere. That I knew of. Maybe the tree would drop a sonnet into my lap. And of course she pulled a magnificent, thick songbook out of her bag.

I pulled out a mostly empty spiral-bound notebook.

KATY'S MAGNIFICENT SONG BOOK

Katy's SONG BOOK

MY MEAGER (MOSTLY EMPTY) POETRY BOOK...

GABBY'S POETRY

Katy: Well, I'm super-jels. Fresh notebooks are the best.

Me: Yeah, I need to work on some new material.

(In-My-Head Me: I need **ANY** material.)

Katy: Hook me up with a rhyme: Back in the day, I was five, it was dope. Seven years pass, I'm twelve and . . .

Me: I've got a whole different scope?

Katy: Oooh, you're good!!

Up until she said that, I had just a few scribbles for my sonnet, but Katy telling me I was good was huge. So was watching her cross things out and move things around and say things aloud to herself.

I realized I'd been trying to write a poem in one big rush, instead of little by little.

I started to fill in my blank spaces, helping Katy here and there with rhymes. I also let my mind wander, like I'd wandered yesterday, and I wound up—yeah, on a baseball field. A metaphorical one. Where I was the ball.

LIFE IS A BALL

I start my journey in an umpire's hand
Or sometimes a bucket of ~~siblings~~ siblings
I am a baseball waiting to land
In   glove. It's not basketball, no dribbling
My work it begins the ~~first~~ first inning hence...
With a throw from the mound to the catcher
I'm stitched together, my insides quite dense
So it must be if I am to soar and to whir
It's my place out here on this field brown and ~~green~~ green
If I'm not there, I'm not sure who I am
And I doth fly through the air like you've never seen
Sometimes I become a grand slam.
So think of me not as just a ball
But as a planet ~~at~~ at the center of the game,
and it all.

I was pretty proud to have used a few old-timey-sounding words. Who knew that I could grow my vocabulary so fast? Being done with the poem felt good. But I wasn't sure that the poem itself **WAS** any good.

> **Bob:** *I can't believe it. She's written an acceptable poem!*
> **Judy:** *A sonnet, no less!*
> **Bob:** *Is this really it? The numbers have been going in her favor, and she's close. Is Gabby Garcia resuming her life winning streak?*
> **Judy:** *Gee, Bob, I hope so. I really don't want to witness any more bummer plays.*

Judy wasn't being very nice. My plays hadn't been total bummers, even if I was getting a little loose with what I called a win. But since Judy was me, I kind of understood.

Katy peeked over the top of my page. "You gonna read that?"

"It needs to sink in," I said, trying to cover it up. What would Katy think of all the old-timey words? Were they lame? I didn't think so but I didn't have a lot to go on. If the only poem I had was silly, and Katy had a massive, intimidating songbook, would it just show the team I was a fraud? "Shakespeare always waited a day to read his stuff out loud."

Katy squinted at me. "Is that true?"

"I don't know," I admitted. I thought about saying "poetic license" but instead I said, "It sounded good, though, right?" Katy cracked up laughing. "G, I'm glad you're on the team." I was, too.

WINS: 7

(a definite win!—and that's, what, four in a row!!)

LOSSES: 8

READ ALOUD FOR A CROWD

Goal: Take my poetry career to the next level.
Action: Read my poem aloud for the talent squad.

Post-Day Analysis:
May 14

After I got home yesterday, my poem was burning a hole in my notebook. Not really; that's kind of a different way of saying this expression my parents use when I have spending money, that it's burning a hole in my pocket. (But wouldn't the money burn up first? Come on, guys.)

I read it and read it and read it and maybe it was all the reading but I thought it was pretty good. Good enough to share.

So today, when lunch period arrived, instead of just plopping down in my usual seat, I stayed standing as some of the squad sat down. I was shifting from foot to foot because I was so excited but also nervous to be sharing my work.

"Do you have to pee, Gabby?" Sophia cocked her head to one side to study me.

"No!" I kind of yelled it, in the way someone who had to go pee probably would. But it was just nerves. I pulled my folded-up poem pages from my back pocket. "I just—I think I have my talent show poem."

"The one you were working on yesterday, G?" Katy asked. She turned to everyone. "She wouldn't let me see it. Said Shakespeare always made things sit a day."

Molly made a squinty face. "That's not true, is it?"

Katy and I shared a glance and cracked up. "Nah," Katy said, "but it sounds like it could be, and Shakes would like that, right, G?" I liked that we had a private joke.

"Shakes? You guys are nuts," Molly said, seeming very big-sistery. "Read your poem, Gabby."

Everyone else nodded and put down their sandwiches. I had the full attention of my audience.

So I started to read.

When I pitch, I try to keep my focus on the plate and not the stands. It can be tempting to look, but really, when you're at the center of the field, you know eyes are on you. You don't have to witness them.

Reading a poem is different because your audience is right

in front of your face. Mine was really close to my face, in fact, since I was standing a few feet away. So I could see every expression they made.

They looked . . . serious.

I thought for a second that it was because they didn't like it. But then I realized that my eyes were misting over—especially when I read that line, "If I'm not there, I'm not sure who I am." Like the baseball in my poem.

The TEAM'S SERIOUSLY SERIOUS REACTIONS TO MY SERIOUS POEM:

MOLLY'S

KATY'S

SOPHIA'S

ARLO'S

COLIN'S

LISA'S — SHE'S A LITTLE SPOOKY! FOR SURE

They were definitely a captive audience. I just hoped they didn't worry too much about my emotional state. I didn't have time for drama with a win streak starting.

I was maybe a bit too loud, because Mario Salamida, walking past on his way to the garbage can, said, "What is that garbage, Gaggy? Guess you can take the Luther Polluter out of the school, but you can't take the pollution out of the person."

I hated hearing that name again, but at least he didn't throw up in the garbage can.

And it doesn't matter what Mario thinks.

I doth did an excellent job, **METHINKS**.

When I was done, no one said anything for a few seconds. They were all nodding slowly, letting my words wash over them. That had to be it. There's no way a poem that had brewed so long couldn't be good.

"So?" I said. The words had had enough time to wash over them.

"It's definitely a poem!" Molly said, and I hoped she wasn't threatened by my talent or interesting words or creativity in being the ball. "Let's hear it for Gabby."

The table clapped for me, and I imagined their applause multiplied by at least 100. I imagined the internet breaking as people tried to vote for me.

This was going to be so great!

I took a little bow, because I'd earned it.

WINS: 8

(five in a row—total streak territory!)

LOSSES: 8 (I'm .500 again!)

REHEARSAL RHYMING

Goal: WIN the talent showcase!!!
Action: Practice, practice, practice.

Post-Day Analysis:
May 15

In sports movies, a lot of times there's a montage of people training to get ready for a big game, and now, with the talent showcase officially less than a week away, all our individual time working was coming together in a practice run of our talent show lineup.

The field hockey team had—no surprise—not made the playoffs, so from here on out, we'd be working on the showcase.

THINGS LESS SURPRISING THAN THE PIPER BELL FIELD HOCKEY TEAM NOT MAKING THE PLAYOFFS

- The earth remaining round

- The sky being blue

- The night being dark

- Baby sloths being adorable

Coach Raddock was more pepped up than I'd ever seen her as she told us about how the showcase would work.

"Okay, squad! We have our lineup set. For the show, you'll each perform your act. Five minutes per! Max! Otherwise, people at home start getting restless. And we want them to vote! And they will!" She was not Calm Yoga Coach anymore. She was Go-Get-'Em Coach now. "The Preteen Talent Showcase website will be live-streaming everyone's act, from our school and the competing schools. We'll have a monitor backstage so we can watch our votes add up."

Our region had four competitors, and voters at home would be able to select and flip between the streams to award points per act. So it was really all about stage presence.

"If you've got their attention, you'll probably get their votes,"

Coach Raddock said. "And we have some big personalities, so I'm not too worried." She smiled at me when she said that last part.

She, unlike Coach Hollylighter, appreciates my big personality!

I wasn't nervous about this at all. Years on the mound had given me confidence when it came to being out in front of lots of people. I wondered if my teammates were up for it. I hoped they were better at being onstage than they were at the field hockey pitch.

But, it turned out, I had nothing to worry about!

So, to go back to what I started with, we were entering the training montage part of our ramp-up to the showcase. In movies, especially sports ones or anything where people are preparing for a big event, there is always a great song and lots of scenes where everyone has a ton of energy and they look unstoppable and **THEY ARE THE MOST EXCITING SCENES** because even if things are a little predictable, those scenes are the part of the movie when I think, "**THEY'RE GONNA WIN!**"

Even if that's not always the case, I love a montage.

BEST MOVIE TRAINING MONTAGES EVER

- *Rocky*

- Major League

- The Karate Kid

- Mulan

- Matilda

- Pitch Perfect

Our montage went something like this:

Molly brings us to tears reading a sad scene from her book! Marilyn lights up the stage—almost literally—with her terrifying but actually educational chemical reaction demonstration. (Yes, she does almost set herself on fire, but it's exciting.) Arlo makes such a great case for why twelve-year-olds should get to vote that I wish he were running for president! Colin's tap routine makes my heart do a little dance along with his rhythm. Dominic projects giant photos across a screen and I feel like I could step inside each one! Grace spray-paints a mural as Sophia does half-pipe skateboard flips in midair. And then Katy practically bursts off the stage with her dancers and we're all singing along to "See the Day." And Lisa Clover . . . well, she makes a rabbit float! It's impressive.

POW!!!

And, somewhere in there, I read my poem and felt 100 percent certain . . .

We had talent!

So much!

"That was a great rehearsal, gang!" Coach Raddock said. "And, Gabby, how lucky we are to have you!"

"You're our good luck charm, G!" Katy said, with a hug.

Yup, a good luck charm. Not a **JINX**!

NEW YORK, GET READY FOR GABBY GARCIA! WIN! WIN! WIN!

WINS: 9
LOSSES: 8
(hey, hey, hey, good-bye LOSSING STREAK!)

THINGS I'M GOING TO DO WHEN
OUR TALENT SQUAD GOES TO NEW YORK

• Rent a paddleboat in Central Park

• Visit all the museums and feel my brain expand three sizes

• Eat pizza in Little Italy

- Smile and wave at everyone I see, because I bet New Yorkers aren't **THAT** rude

- Go to the top of the Empire State building and look for Yankee Stadium

- Eat a lot of hot dogs from carts

- Eat a hot dog at Yankee Stadium

- Eat a hot dog at Citi Field

- Eat a baseball-helmet sundae at Yankee Stadium

- Eat a baseball-helmet sundae at Citi Field

- See a Broadway show

- Actually, scratch the Broadway show in favor of more baseball games

- Probably get another hot dog . . .

- At a baseball game

THAT'S THE WAY
THE MUFFIN CRUMBLES

Goal: Feel completely at ease with my decision to leave the playoff-bound baseball team.

Action: Prove to myself that I'm in the right place by assisting the talent squad as we raise money for our showcase.

Post-Day Analysis:
May 20

I'm sick in my bed, writing this, which shows how it all went.

Not well.

I thought, I really thought, that if I just put my Gabby-Garcia-all into being on the field hockey team, or the talent squad, and into being a poet, and if we could win the showcase and go to New York and be on TV and everything that went with that . . . well, I thought I would feel like a winner again.

But today I figured something out: it was never just about winning. It was about being on the baseball team. It was about being a baseball player.

This is how I figured it out. Not that there's anything I can do about it now.

Today, the talent squad had to sell things in the school cafeteria. Just a little fund-raiser to pay for our banner that would hang during the showcase. We were selling gluten-free health muffins.

THINGS TO SELL TO MIDDLE SCHOOLERS
IF YOU REALLY DON'T WANT TO RAISE MONEY

• Socks freshly removed from the feet of your uncle who plays squash

• Pickled beets in Ziploc bags

• Bonus visits to the dentist

• Itchy dress-up clothing grandmas think is "darling"

• Gluten-free "health muffins"

THINGS TO SELL TO MIDDLE SCHOOLERS
IF YOU REALLY DO WANT TO RAISE MONEY

• Custom-created ice cream cookie sandwiches

And, yup, that was what the baseball team was selling at the table next to ours. Our table with health muffins.

I was so angry. And sad. And hungry for an ice cream cookie sandwich.

I'd just started to feel really good about my choice to be part of the talent squad, and now this happened!

Devon, Mario, Bobby, and Madeleine—who still eye-balled me like I might just come running at her nose with a hammer— were behind their table. "Be Sweet! Help Us Get Playoff Ready!" was written on the sign they'd made. Johnny was helping the team give change to all its customers. He seemed to be avoiding eye contact with me as much as I was with him.

But I was trying to avoid it with everyone. Because there we were—me, Katy, Molly, and Arlo—working a table with a sign painted by Grace Chang that said "Our Goodness Depends on Your Goodness!" It looked beautiful, but it wasn't very clear what it meant.

And, of course, no one wanted a **HEALTH MUFFIN**, goodness or not. Molly and her mom had made them and each one seemed to weigh twelve pounds. Not good, muffin-y pounds. More like someone had poured sand into a muffin tin and sprinkled it with rocks.

SAND MUFFIN OF DOOM

Meanwhile, the baseball team's ice cream cookie sandwiches were custom-made—you chose your cookies and the flavor of ice cream you wanted. And then they bundled it in a little bag with the Penguin baseball logo on it so that it wouldn't drip on your hands. They were melty, dreamy goodness. Almost ice-cream-sundae-in-a-little-helmet caliber.

THE MOST dreamy ICE CREAM COOKIE SANDWICH EVER

"Whoa, Gaggy, you really took some steps down in the world," Mario said as I tried to use ESP to lure people away from the baseball team's never-ending cookie line. The only kids in our line were a few members of the Ecology Club and some of Katy's fans, who were only buying cookies out of true devotion to her.

"Mario, you don't have to be a jerk," Devon said, and caught my eye. I looked away from her. I didn't want to jinx the cookie creations, even if I kind of did. And I definitely didn't want Devon's pity.

Let her be a winner. I was a good luck charm. And a poet. And not a jinx. I told myself these things, in my head, on repeat.

Still, my stomach was aching again. And I hadn't even eaten one of the muffins. It was just, seeing our food side by side with the baseball team's food made me feel like maybe I'd made the wrong choice, that I wasn't getting my winning streak back after all.

But it wasn't even that.

Devon was oiling her mitt. Baseball mitts need to be oiled so they stay nice and bendy for wrapping around a ball. I missed the smell of that oil. Even though I'd been wearing my mitt while I wrote, I hadn't been oiling it. I'd been neglecting my mitt.

They'd decorated their table with a baseball bat laid horizontally and two brand-new baseballs on each side of it, and I wanted to pick up one of the balls to feel the red stitches along its seams.

Then I saw a grass stain on the back of Mario's jersey. And I'd gotten plenty of grass stains on my clothes during field hockey, but this was a **BASEBALL FIELD** grass stain. Why did Mario get to have a grass stain and I didn't?

And, okay, the ice cream cookies looked delicious compared to the muffins. The ice cream cookies were the dessert I'd have chosen. (Okay, so everyone would have.) But still . . .

They were just desserts, but all the poetry I'd been reading had started to make me feel like this was symbolic. And then my stomach clenched up and I started to breathe too quick and I just wanted to get out of there.

"I, um, gotta go. To the nurse's office."

"Are you okay, G? You look kinda green," Katy said, putting a friendly hand on my shoulder.

I felt kind of green. With envy.

"I'll be okay," I said, not knowing if it was true.

And I ran out of the cafeteria.

In the hall, Johnny caught up with me. "What's wrong?"

"Nothing," I lied, again. I was lying all over the place.

"It's not a big deal if you don't sell many muffins," he said. "I'm sure you'll still have a talent show."

He wasn't getting it. But why would he? I'd told him I'd made the right choice. I'd been lying to everyone.

"Look, you don't have to be so nice to me," I snapped. "You should get back to the baseball team, where you belong." *And I don't,* I thought.

"You could probably still come back," Johnny said. But I was already walking away from him. From baseball. Where I belonged, too.

It sounded perfect. And so simple. I was meant to play baseball; why would I not? It wasn't even about the winning.

I just wanted to **PLAY**. Baseball. Even if I had to ride the bench most of the time, I wanted to be there. Losing at baseball would be better than winning at poetry. I wished I'd realized it sooner. But besides the fact the team didn't want me, I had a team that did. Full of friends who'd probably be disappointed if I just gave up on them now. So didn't I belong there even more?

I started this playbook because I really believed you could turn anything into a win if you thought about it the right way. For maybe the first time in my life, I couldn't even see a way to turn this into a win.

Win. That word again. Was I winning?

The nurse called my dad and I went home from school early. I barely got out the fake "I'll be fine" when my dad asked what was the matter.

I've been lying in bed since then.

And I've turned down all the things that usually cheer me up—pitching practice with my dad, watching the Braves game, chatting online with Diego, talking to Louie in her office—none of them sounded good at all.

The only good news is, lying around in bed feeling like I'm having a crisis feels very poet-like. I know I have to rally. I can't go back to the baseball team. Those days are long behind me. But if the talent squad doesn't win, then everything I've done will have been for nothing.

It almost makes me wish I'd never experienced such an amazing win streak, because no matter what I do, I don't feel like I'll ever quite get it back. And even if I am getting it back, is it the **WRONG** win streak?

WINS: 9
LOSSES: 8
CONFUSING CONUNDRUMS
THAT MAKE ME QUESTION EVERYTHING: 1
(feels like more, though)

REPLAY:
DON'T-MAKE-PLANS PLAY

This is another surprise play. Or just a surprise.

I've tried to keep my playbook about strategy and goals, but maybe by recording some of the surprises, I'll learn from them in the future. I can only hope, anyway.

There I was, minding my own business in algebra. Like really minding it. There were only a few more weeks of school left, so I needed good grades and I needed to just, maybe, get this year over with. I wanted to be excited so I was trying my best to do that. But I'd been in crisis mode since the fund-raiser and doubting everything. I knew what I wanted to do—play baseball. But I also knew what I didn't want to do. (Disappoint the talent squad.)

I wanted a sign.

Instead, I got a note. It was definitely for me, because my name was right on the front of it. In really lousy handwriting.

I looked around, wondering who might have passed it to me. My first thought was Johnny, who I was still avoiding. Maybe he was apologizing. It was possible, even though I knew he hadn't done anything wrong. He'd just been echoing that little voice in my head that told me I never should have left baseball. Even for the potential glory of winning the talent show.

But when I turned behind me to look at him, his head was bent over his book.

And then I saw Devon, with her arm all slinged up. "Read it," she mouthed, pointing at the note.

I unfolded it. She must have written it with her bum arm because the handwriting was super-wobbly and she'd only fit about four words on each line.

My first thought was, it was almost like a poem. A really weird poem by a robot or something, but still a poem.

Second thought? Whoa.

It was kind of what I wanted to happen all along. Not the part where Devon sprained her arm. I didn't want anyone to get

Gabby—

I won't be able
to pitch in the
big playoff game on
Saturday. I sprained my
pitching arm scooping ice cream.
(Don't ask.)

I think you
need to take my place.
Other pitchers we have
are not as good as you.
Playoffs = important.

Think about it.

Talked to Coach and
she is on board.

Devon

hurt. Especially scooping ice cream. How did **THAT** happen?

But I had wanted the team to come to me, to say it needed me and my winning ability. And here it was.

Plus, Coach signed off? How did that happen?

I spent the rest of algebra feeling very antsy.

Because I wanted to hear what Coach had said about me. Did she admit she was wrong about me all along? Was it a dramatic moment for her?

Because the game is Saturday. The talent showcase is also Saturday!

Because I could do a lot of things but I couldn't be in two places at once.

Finally, the bell rang, signaling the end of class, and I almost jumped out of my chair. Actually, I kind of did and smashed right into Johnny Madden, sending his books and mine flying everywhere.

AWKWARD.
ALSO, OUCH!

"Careful," he said. "Or you'll sprain your arm, too."

It took me a second to realize he was talking about Devon's arm and also expressing concern for mine.

"What?"

"To pitch. No, never mind. Just talk to Devon."

Did he have something to do with this? Probably. But he was being strange. Everything was strange.

He picked up his things and hurried out the door. I jogged to catch up with Devon, who was already in the hall.

"I got your note," I told her.

"I know," she said, with several blinks and a look like she didn't have time for me. Even though she wrote the note. "I saw you read it."

Devon and I didn't exactly have that rapport thing yet. Maybe we wouldn't ever.

"Are you gonna do it?" she asked me. "You'd better say yes. It's the playoffs."

I took a deep breath. **OF COURSE** I wanted to do it! But I had the talent showcase. And, if we won, New York. But who knew if we'd win? I had no idea what we were up against.

Bob: *Wow, this is big, Judy! Big! Who'd have thought the baseball team would come to Gabby, after all her struggles to find her place with them? She must love this!*

Judy: But she has a place, Bob! The talent squad! She can't let them down.

Bob: But Gabby is baseball. Baseball **IS** Gabby.

They were both right. And it was killing me.

"I thought you thought I was a jinx," I said.

Devon stopped blinking to roll her eyes. "Whatever. I was being a jerk. I was angry." She didn't say more and I didn't ask. Because I knew I had been a different kind of jerk by quitting the team so quickly. I had wanted to be the most important, most valuable, most **EVERYTHING** on the Penguins from the second I stepped on the field, and I'd let it get in the way of being true to myself. I'd been so focused on getting back the perfect life that I hadn't stopped to wonder if it was the **RIGHT** life.

Devon sighed and looked irritated. "He said you wouldn't be sure," she said.

"Who said that?"

"Johnny. It was his idea. After I sprained my arm, he told Coach Hollylighter you were our best chance to win the playoff game. He said you just needed the right encouragement."

It was a metaphor of the first degree because the news hit me like a ton of bricks.

Oh, wait, that was a simile.

I didn't totally understand why Johnny seemed to be my biggest fan after knowing me for such a short time period, but the why wasn't important. He'd been pulling for me for a while now. And also nagging me, but it wasn't like he was wrong. I **DID** miss baseball.

"And Coach Hollylighter was excited about the idea?"

"As excited as she gets," Devon said with a smirk. "She pretends to be all business but she likes to win. So do I."

I guessed Coach Hollylighter and Devon and I had that in common.

I didn't really know what to say to any of this, but when I closed my eyes, I saw myself . . . . on the mound, folding my glove in and out, waiting to throw the first pitch of the game. Not at the talent show.

Nope. I wanted to be back in the game. A big game. Gosh, any game.

The squad had been good before I came along. They'd be good without me. And wouldn't Piper Bell herself want me to pursue my true talent? My true love?

"You know you want to say yes," Devon said, reading my mind.

So I did. And I couldn't wait for the game. But that didn't

make anything else easier. The talent squad had become my friends, and I was going to let them down. We have rehearsal in just under an hour. (I'm sweatily writing this in the empty atrium, but I think I'm sweating for other reasons.)

This was definitely a no-win scenario.

THE EXTRACTION

Goal: Quit the talent show. By telling the truth.
Action: Make the announcement at the exact right time so that it causes the least damage to the team/squad.

Post-Day Analysis
May 24, Part Two

TIMING.
IS.
EVERYTHING.

Especially when it comes to bad things. Or that's what I was telling myself. Not that being in the game was a bad thing: it was the right thing. It was the being-true-to-me thing. But that didn't make quitting the talent show any easier.

In baseball, when you have to pull a player from the

roster—for an injury or a family crisis or a case of the yips—you usually have someone else on the roster to substitute for them. In the case of the talent show, there was no one to sub for me—and I was the good luck charm. If I lost my good luck charm before a big game, I'd be really freaked out.

But I'd also rather learn that a great player or my coach was going to be out of the game right before the game—or as close to right before the game as possible—because the less time I had to think about it, the less time I would have to worry about it.

LESS WORRY = BETTER.

Which works, because there is only one night before the talent showcase and the playoff game. At Coach Hollylighter's office, I poked my head in the door.

"Coach Hollylighter?"

She looked up from her own playbook, where I could see she was making a lineup for Saturday.

I saw my name next to the words "Starting Pitcher" and my heart leapt around happily. Imagining taking the mound again made me think of a thousand poems, all at once.

SPOTTED MY NAME ON COACH'S LIST

PLAYERS LIST

GABBI GARCIA

But I tried to act casual. I was afraid of seeming like I had a big ego or bad rapport or whatever else Coach Hollylighter worried I might have. I also felt really guilty for how happy I was. I was counting on the talent squad to understand.

"Hi, Gabby, good to see you," she said, and smiled.

It threw me. It wasn't like she'd ever been happy to see me before.

"Hi, I'm, um, playing Saturday. I'm here for my uniform."

She pointed to a chair where a uniform was folded up. "That's the same size as your old one," she said. As I picked it up, she added, "So did you work everything out with your talent squad? They understand?"

Gulp.

"Yup!" I said. "All taken care of."

"That's great. You wouldn't want it hanging over your head before the game. Or at all, really. It's considerate you told them right away."

Ugh. More guilt rumbled in my belly. I took my uniform and thanked her, trying not to show how anxious I was about this.

By the time I got to rehearsal, the lump in my throat was about the size of a baseball. The woozy feeling in my stomach was worse than ever.

"G, you're here! I was all, 'We can't start without our good luck charm,' and then you show up!" Katy shouted from the stage.

Everyone said hi to me in a chorus and then Coach Raddock even came up to me and added, "How amazing is it that if it hadn't been for that day in algebra, none of this would have happened? It's such great fate."

Oh no. All their happiness was just making it worse.

Coach Raddock called everyone to order and we took places backstage, waiting to rehearse our numbers. Maybe I could just practice this one last time and **THEN** tell them?

But suddenly I just blurted it out.

"Um, I won't be here tomorrow . . ." I said it fast, like ripping off a Band-Aid, except it was like when a little piece of the scab comes off with it and starts to bleed again.

"Wait . . . what?" Katy asked. Her voice was loud and sharp and she spun around to look at me. "You won't be here? And you're just telling us now? You don't look like you're dying. So what's the deal?"

Everyone looked at me. None of them looked happy anymore.

"It's complicated. It's, well, I'm a baseball player and the team needs me to pitch. For the playoff game," I said. "Their best pitcher hurt her arm and pitching is kind of my thing—my real thing—and . . ."

"Wait, so you're going to bail on us for the baseball team?" Molly asked, sounding more hurt than angry. She trailed off as an "aha!" look sprang to her face. "We should have known after that poem! You're in love with baseball. Not poetry. No wonder you were all teary-eyed reading it! You lied and now you're **BAILING** on us."

This was all going even worse than I imagined. "Yes. But not bail. I mean, it's just that the game is the same time as the talent showcase and I just can't be both places at once. And I didn't lie . . . I just—I was trying something new."

"You lied. Plus, instead of sticking with the team you've been on for the past month, you chose the baseball team," Sophia said. "Total bailfest."

"Wow. This is cuh-lassic. Who does that? Just ditches her friends? Or maybe we're not her friends. **NOT. AT. ALL**," Katy said. "I wanna be a star, too. We all do. But, what, you just leave because you can be a bigger star there? The baseball team can have you. I mean, until someone better comes along."

She stormed off and I thought the worst was over until I saw Molly's face. Her angry, angry face.

"Whatever, guys, let's just let Gabby go," she said. "I mean, isn't she kind of the weakest link anyway?"

Molly said that. Molly, who seemed like a big sister to me.

"What? I thought you liked my poem." My voice was little.

Katy had stopped walking and was looking at me again.

From across the stage, she said, "Yeah, I called you the good luck charm to be nice. Anyone who listens knows you're not much of a poet. I mean, 'Life's a Ball'? I've read better grocery lists."

"Team, let's not be so unkind," Coach Raddock said, even though her eyes looked disappointed, too.

"I wanted to be part of the talent showcase," I said. "I never really wrote poems before. But I really was trying."

"Why would you lie?" Marilyn asked, her eyes widening.

"I was on a win streak at my old school because before I came here I played baseball and I was good and then here I was a Luther Polluter and I was a jinx on the baseball team and then I met you guys and the talent showcase sounded so great like I could get my life back on track and win something great and . . ." I trailed off, out of breath, because I knew whatever I said wasn't going to make things better. Sometimes I can read the way a game is going to go and know when there's no saving it. But still, in a soft voice, I added, "And baseball is just my thing . . . my real thing."

But no one heard me, or they didn't care.

"Come on, guys, Gabby probably needs to get back to her **REAL** team," Katy said. "We were just temporary friends on her brief losing streak."

And I almost said, "They're not my team! You are!"

But the truth is, I didn't know if I was ever on either team, not all the way.

And I did want a win. I wanted everything to make sense again and to know I was in the right place, doing everything just perfect.

This did not feel perfect.

As everyone turned their backs on me, I tried to remember that I had turned my back on them first.

Then it got worse.

Dad picked me up from school. I was about to tell him how awful the last hour had been when he said, "The Collinses had to take Dumpster to the hospital today. He started retch-ing this morning and was still sick around lunchtime. He's at the vet's."

Uh-oh. I tried to think of what I gave Dumpster to eat this morning, but I couldn't see why it would have made him sick. It was chicken mole from last night. It didn't smell funny or anything.

Then Dad added: "The interesting thing was, they said that it looked like Dumpster had eaten some mole sauce, like we had for dinner last night. There's cocoa in it. Dogs shouldn't have it."

We were at a stoplight and Dad turned to look at me and it was clear he knew **THE UGLY TRUTH**.

"Where would a dog get mole sauce? I didn't throw away

our leftovers," he said. "They were in your lunch."

I was quiet.

"How many lunches have you fed to Dumpster?"

"Um . . . ," I started to answer.

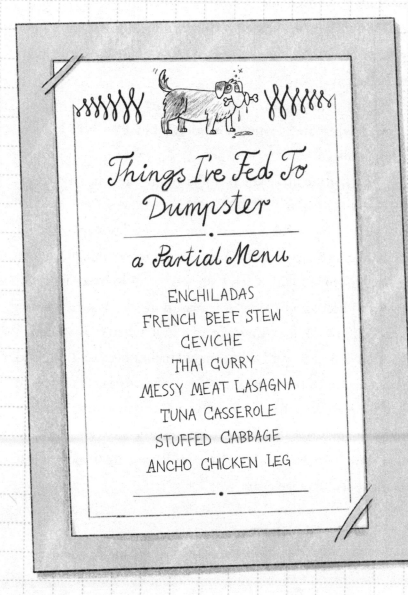

Things I've Fed To Dumpster

a Partial Menu

ENCHILADAS

FRENCH BEEF STEW

CEVICHE

THAI CURRY

MESSY MEAT LASAGNA

TUNA CASSEROLE

STUFFED CABBAGE

ANCHO CHICKEN LEG

"This is why we keep running out of peanut butter and turkey so fast, isn't it?" My dad hit the steering wheel. "I thought Peter was having a growth spurt."

"I . . ." There was absolutely nothing good to say to this.

"Gabby, was my food embarrassing you?"

"No," I said. My voice was little and thin; the voice I got when I lied. Dad knew the voice. And he knew better than to believe it.

He was really quiet. I was really quiet.

So I whispered a tiny "I'm sorry," but Dad was looking straight ahead.

"I try hard to make you feel like you can tell me anything," he said, eyes still on the road.

I didn't know what to say, but I knew he was right. I'd always told my dad and Louie everything. I thought about what Diego had said when I started going to Piper Bell and wanted the baseball team to come to me, how sometimes it was okay to ask for things, or to admit what you wanted. I hadn't wanted to ask Dad for new lunches because I worried about making a problem, and solving the problem on my own had seemed like what a winner would do. But I was learning in too many ways that I didn't have all the answers.

I think it's time to stop tallying wins and losses now. I just want to feel like me again.

SEVENTH-INNING STRETCH

No, I haven't skipped anything.

This seventh-inning stretch is a **METAPHOR**.

(I guess I have learned something from my poet days. Days that seem so far behind me now that I almost expect to see them turn up again on the horizon. Even though they were just earlier today. Also, yikes, that is bad. Maybe I am a bad poet.)

But with the seventh-inning-stretch thing, I'm totally on base.

Casual fans, the kind of people who want their team to win, sure, but who won't be knocked out if they lose—well, they think the seventh-inning stretch is fun. Everyone gets up and sings and sways and the song mentions peanuts and everything! Peanuts are fun, right? (Except for people who are allergic, in which case, not fun.)

But to me, if my team is the losing team—and especially when I'm losing and playing at **HOME**—the seventh-inning stretch is nothing more than long minutes of torture set to a cheerful song.

There's even a line in it, "**ROOT, ROOT, ROOT FOR THE HOME TEAM / IF THEY DON'T WIN IT'S A SHAME.**"

But if I'm the home team, down several runs and having a thousand or so people singing that? (Or even a hundred or so? Or twelve?) That I'm going to be a **SHAME** for losing? Yeah, it stinks.

So, if I'm the home team right now—and I am, it's my playbook—this is the seventh-inning stretch . . .

And I'm **LOSING BIG TIME**.

It is a shame.

Everything is my fault.

I have no friends left.

I'm to blame for my neighbor's sick dog.

I have a dad who thinks he can't really trust me to tell him stuff. And that I'm embarrassed of him.

And maybe I'm going to be pitching in a baseball game soon, as a starter, in a big game, and that's what I wanted from the beginning, but with all this other stuff around it, I'm really worried. It's not even a yips kind of worried. It's a worse, sick feeling that's burrowed in my stomach and that makes me want to hide under my covers forever.

But tomorrow's game could cost the Penguins their whole season.

And it's already cost me my friends.

So everyone else can go ahead and sing and eat peanuts but I need to figure something out, and fast.

THE PICKING-UP-THE-PIECES

Goal: Fix **EVERYTHING**.
Action: Do **EVERYTHING**.

Post-Day Analysis
May 24, Part Three (Late Edition)

I did hide under my covers for a few minutes, clutching this playbook, hoping for the right ideas. I let my mind wander. And of course, it wandered onto a ball field.

In baseball, when all hope was lost for me on the mound (and it didn't happen often but it had happened), I knew that a reliever could come in and—hopefully—reverse the bad.

It was called a save.

I really needed a save now.

The problem with life versus baseball is, I can't just have someone take over for me when things are awful.

SAVES-THE-DAY-
GABBY*

CAN BE WHEREVER GABBY #1 CANNOT!

READY FOR ANYTHING

S.T.D.G.

HAPPY TO HELP

NEVER LETS YOU DOWN

*REMINDER: THIS PERSON DOES NOT EXIST!

Darn, why couldn't life be like baseball?

HOW LIFE WOULD BE BETTER
IF IT WERE LIKE BASEBALL

- People to cheer for you when things were going well

- People to cheer for you when things were not going well

- Cool furry mascots to pep you up, no matter what was going on

- Rain delays to put things on hold when conditions weren't great

- Relievers to take over for you when you had an off day

- Mostly, rules that made sense **ALL THE TIME**

The only one who can save me is me. But a better me, who won't make the same mistakes.

Hmm. **A BETTER ME WHO WON'T MAKE THE SAME MISTAKES** . . . How can I do everything while also being just one person? Maybe be the better me?

Bob: Judy, I think Gabby is onto something here.

Judy: Bob, she's so close. I think she can save things.

Bob: It's going to take a lot of work.

Judy: Work, yes. Plus inner strength, and a lot of apologizing.

Bob: She doesn't have much time!

So wait, maybe I do have a reliever . . . and it's me?

As Bob and Judy hashed things out in my head, my little Gabbys were a disorganized mess, jumping around under my skin, trying to decide what to do first. Mostly, they were just crashing into each other, making me a sweaty mess.

It was my body's way of telling me that I could only do one thing at a time.

Sigh.

But I can be the better me. I'd been so focused on getting a win **FOR ME**, and doing everything just right **FOR ME**, that I forgot there was a whole **TEAM** to consider. Not just my talent show team. But everyone I'd sort of ignored or overlooked because I'd been so concerned with getting **MY LIFE PERFECT**.

It was like Johnny had said (and he was one of the people I'd ignored): if you're actually playing the game, there are no perfect seasons. And maybe no perfect lives. Just good ones where everyone you knew wasn't mad at you. And where you didn't worry about being perfect but about being true to yourself. 'Cause what was the point of being perfect if everything you did was for some fake version of yourself? Fake perfect wasn't worth it.

Okay, what would better me do? I was trying to answer that when Diego called. So I got derailed as I unraveled the whole story for him, but he understood (because he's my best friend) and did say one thing that made sense: "You have to start at home." Just like in baseball? Get it?

So, yup, first I needed to patch things up with my dad.

I didn't really know what I could do besides apologize again.

It wasn't an exciting play but it was the right one.

My dad was in the kitchen, making dinner. But not the way he usually made dinner, where the counters were an explosion of spices and bowls and creative chaos and music or a ball game playing in the background.

It was quiet as he opened the oven and slid in a dish of enchiladas. He looked sad and not like himself. It was my fault.

I sat at the counter in the same stool where I always sit when we're having a talk. I waited for him to look up.

When he finally did, I said, "I'm sorry, Dad."

It wasn't enough at all. It was like a pitch that doesn't even reach the plate. Saves-the-Day Gabby didn't have the tricks up her sleeve that I needed.

But then my dad surprised me.

"No, I'm sorry," he said. "I should have been paying more attention. I knew something was up when you left the baseball team. Have you been having a hard time at Piper Bell?"

I thought about this, and the answer—at least for the past few weeks, since I joined up with the field hockey team/talent squad—was more or less no.

But also yes.

So I shrugged, the universal gesture for when the answer to something is yes and no. "It's just different," I said.

Dad nodded, getting it. "You've always had a place and then you didn't, huh?"

"I guess. And things were going so great at Luther and it all got taken away," I said.

"You know, you can just tell me these things, even when life is busy." He let out a sigh and smiled a little. "And it doesn't seem like you're doing **SO** bad. You've seemed happy, even after that loss." (I never wrote about it but I did have my parents come to the last field hockey game because I figured why not? And we lost, of course, but it hadn't bothered me because I'd been so fired up to write poetry. For the talent showcase, which they **DON'T** know about.) I'd have to tell him about the talent showcase. And the playoff game. But later. First, I needed to check on my friend.

"Is Dumpster going to be okay?"

Dad nodded. "They caught it in time. But you still need to apologize to the Collinses. I thought about making them some cookies. You can bring them when you go talk to them."

"None for Dumpster."

"No, we'll whip up some doggie biscuits when he's better."

"I'll help," I said. I knew I had a lot to do but making cookies couldn't hurt, right?

"You bet you will." Dad grinned. "And you can tell me what else is going on with you."

As we set to work on the cookies for the Collinses, I told Dad everything. About baseball and the weird field hockey team and the real reasons why I started to write poetry.

"And here I thought you were just taking up my word-smith genius," Dad said.

"Well, I do like it. I'm just not a genius at it," I said. "But the team, and the talent show, I like doing that. It's just, I really want to pitch this game."

My dad nodded. "Of course you do," he said. "And it sounds like even if you left the baseball team for the wrong reasons, you wound up with the right friends."

"They're not my friends anymore," I said, thinking of how angry Katy and Molly had been.

"You'd be surprised what people will forgive you for if you're just honest," Dad said. "And bring cookies."

There were two pans of cookies in the oven and four more ready for the stove by the time I told him the full, *full* story. And once they were all baked, we went outside so I could practice my pitching for tomorrow.

It wasn't right away, but around my third or fourth pitch, when I went into my windup, that I could almost **FEEL** all the ickiness sort of fall away from me. I was calm. As I let go of the ball and threw a fast one to my dad's waiting glove, it was almost as though all the little Gabbys came together into one Gabby again and the yips and the panic and the sick feeling just stopped. I was just me again.

"What are you thinking, kid?" my dad asked, tossing the ball back to me.

"That the problem is, I can't be everything at once. And I can't do everything at once. But I want to," I said.

"Well, Gabs, when you can't do everything, you do what you can."

And I decided, for the right reasons, that I wasn't going to keep score on my life anymore, as long as I was just being me.

May 24, Later
Small Ball

No set goal, no set strategy, but a **SERIES** of things.

Whew. I think I have a plan. And I haven't given up on the playbook. Not at all, but until tomorrow, I think I just need to play things as they go along. (And record them, of course. Posterity!)

So a lot of people think baseball is all about home runs.

And a lot of it is. Because home runs are fun and exciting and they put points on the board right away.

They're a big deal.

But small ball is different.

Instead of getting the big hits to round the bases all at once, teams try to get runners on and move them, batter by batter. Because not every team has a power hitter like Mario Salamida (who, again, can't get a hit off me).

But small ball just shows that it's not always big things that accomplish a lot. Sometimes, it's moving things in the right direction little by little.

Kind of like apologizing to a group of people you let down.

I'm writing this before bed, hoping for a good night's sleep, after realizing there's no home run of apologies I can give the talent squad. I can't parachute out of the sky onto the stage and say sorry and make everyone vote for them and have them all be grateful to me. I can't clone myself so one Gabby can play in the baseball game while one shows up at the talent showcase. And I can't say no to pitching this game. I just can't. Someday, I'll get my friends to understand that.

But I can at least get on base, from an apology standpoint.

Haikus are my base hit.

Haikus are three-line poems that are only seventeen syllables—five in the first line, seven in the second, and five in the third.

Maybe they're the small ball of poetry.

Well, not exactly, but they're short and have a form I can follow. Already followed, actually. I wrote these for the team and I'm going to leave them backstage tomorrow, with cookies—they really do work wonders; I've eaten six tonight—to show that I may not be able to be *there* for them but I'm *there* for them.

♪ Katy ♪

WHEN YOU SEE THE DAY
REMEMBER THAT YOUR SMILE
SHOULD BE SEEN WITH YOU.

✳ Molly ✳

STORIES SHOULD BE TOLD
SPEAK LOUDLY AND BE VERY CLEAR
AND WORDS COME TO LIFE.

Sophia

YOU'RE DARING AND COOL
TREAT EVERY STUNT LIKE IT'S
MUSIC TO YOUR EARS.

Arlo

YOUR POINTS ARE SMARTEST
WITH A PAUSE HERE, A STOP THERE
TO LET THEM SINK IN.

Marilyn

BRAINS, YOU HAVE THEM (LOTS)
BUT BE EXTRA CAREFUL ALWAYS
DON'T GO UP IN FLAMES.

Lisa

HOW DO YOU DO IT?
I GUESS YOU SHOULDN'T TELL ME
FLOATING BUNNY. WHOA.

They're small starts but they're something. And if things were reversed, and someone wrote one for me, it would help. At least a little.

Little by little is way better than nothing at all.

I hope.

THE NO "I" IN TEAM

Goal: Win! (I think.)

Action: Be true to myself. Which is harder than it sounds. It turns out, my self has a lot of sides. Plus, there are people besides myself to think about. I haven't always been good at that. Life is kind of like a team sport. You can't just have one happy player. I'm definitely getting away from the action part of this play. But it's my playbook and one thing I know for sure now is that some plays aren't clear-cut. And being myself isn't always clear-cut but it's the most important play I've got. And, whew, well, time to see what happens.

Pre-Game Analysis:
May 25

I got to Piper Bell more than an hour before the game. The school was quiet.

I headed to the school auditorium, where the talent squad would perform and be filmed. On a table backstage, right under the bulletin board with the showcase lineup where I knew they'd see them, I set up my haikus (folded, with each squad member's name on it) and a platter of cookies, my apology starter. It was a stretch to hope that they'd **LIKE** the haikus. The cookies should help.

Only feeling the tiniest bit better, I went to the locker room to dress for the game.

Even though I was still shaky about all this life stuff, I felt that same calm I had pitching with my dad. After the last couple days, I finally understood something: it was only a game. It was a huge game and an exciting game and one I wanted to play. And to win.

But the big deal was that I was going to get to play again.

Plus, I was finally getting that I could only win so much. Sometimes things were going to get in the way of it. Things like asbestos. Or the yips. Or even sometimes just plain screwing up and throwing the wrong pitch at the wrong time. Trying so hard to make everything perfect for myself had only made things **HARD**.

I was having an epiphany.

I read about them, and the definition is long and full of words like "manifestation," but the simple version is this:

Epiphanies are basically lightning bolts of feeling that just shoot from the sky and make everything clear.

I couldn't decide if having an epiphany was good or bad right before a huge game with the Penguins.

Deep breath.

I just needed to pitch this game.

I needed—okay, wanted—to win this game. (Even though it is not important from an epiphany standpoint, it was still the right thing to aim for, correct?)

Then I needed to make a grand gesture to the talent squad to make sure they know how important they are to me. (I mean, the haikus were a gesture but they're only seventeen sylla-bles. Hardly grand. Especially from a bad poet like me.) I wasn't going to go to New York with them if I wasn't in the show-case, but that didn't matter as much.

Prizes and glory are just little things.

I wondered if I could lead them in some group epiphany that came with a balloon and confetti drop? An "I'm sorry" epiphany.

A TOTAL GROUP EPIPHANY

I was imagining what that might look like when Devon came into the locker room.

"Hi," she said. Blink blink blink. "You're here early."

"Hey," I said.

We were quiet for a minute. Maybe not even a whole minute but long enough that it felt like a long time. Especially because Devon kept doing the blinking thing.

"So, I've been wanting to ask, did you quit just 'cause I called you a jinx?" Blink blink blink. "That was kinda weird."

"No," I said. "It was part of it, I guess. But it was more complicated than that."

"Hmm," she said as she slowly put her screwed-up arm through the sleeve in her jersey. "I might have quit, too. I always want to be the best. My mom says it's because I'm the oldest child but I say it's because I'm the best child."

I laughed. She was kind of funny. And she smiled and looked less like a tough cowboy for a change.

"Why wouldn't you want to be the best?" I asked. "It's kind of the best, right?"

Now she laughed. "I don't think Coach Hollylighter will tell anyone they're the best, ever." Devon smirked.

"I know!" I said. "It's extra-hard because my old coach always did. I was the Golden Child."

"That's pretty fancy," she said. "I should probably take back that I asked you to pitch for me today."

She stared at me like I was a batter she had to strike out, and for a second, I thought she was going to take off her wrist brace and say, "Yeah, so forget it! I healed faster just to keep you out of the game!"

But then she smiled again. "But I want to win, so I guess I had to ask a Golden Child. That's kinda weird, though. Sounds like a shiny baby."

"Yeah, if I were really golden, it'd be hard to move my arms," I said.

We were cracking up together as the rest of the girls on the team started to funnel in. Madeleine just shot us a look and said, "Laugh all you want, but watch my nose today."

"And get the win," Devon added, suddenly serious.

"I will," I said. If they only knew how many things I had to make happen today . . .

Well, it would be more epiphanies than anyone could handle. And with that, I'm tucking this playbook away to join the rest of the team on the field. Oh boy . . .

REPLAY: GAME DAY

We were playing the Franklin Middle Firecrackers.

They were good. Obviously; they were in the playoffs with us. I'd always wanted to play them when I was at Luther but they weren't in our conference.

But I was a Penguin now.

The rest of the Penguins were nervous. Not about me, even though Madeleine seemed to subconsciously touch her nose every time I got within five feet of her. But there were definitely some big-game jitters. Ryder Mills was gulping water noisily and then chewing on the edge of the paper cup. Samuel Jinkins kept wiping his palms on his uniform. Mario was picking up bat after bat as if testing them but grunting at each one like he was upset with them. Madeleine was kicking the chain-link front of the dugout with her cleats as Danny Pettuci told her again and again to stop doing that.

Even Devon, who wasn't playing, flipped a mitt over in her lap like a coin she was playing heads-or-tails with. Johnny, who I still hadn't spoken to, kept ruffling the pages of his stats log.

But I was calm. There were no Gabby-yips. Plus, Bob and Judy were on a lunch break or something because my mind was clear.

Even calm, I couldn't help but get a charge from the excitement of the stands filling with people. I saw my dad and Louie and Peter close to the front of our bleachers. The sky was cloudless and the breeze was light.

It was the perfect day for a baseball game.

Coach Hollylighter read the lineup with me at starting pitcher. When she said my name, Mario groaned. Madeleine gave me a weird look out of the corner of her eye. Lailah Howard, another pitcher who was not as good as Devon, kind of side-eyed me. I didn't exactly feel welcomed by the team, but then again, I had been the one to quit. So I smelled the air, that before-the-game grass, and told myself to be good enough that they'd be glad to have me.

Ryder and Devon were the only ones who gave me five. Over the top of his log, Johnny made a shy thumbs-up. I returned it, still not knowing how to say sorry to someone who seemed to have known where I was supposed to be all along. I'd been kind of mean to him.

Turning to look out at the crowd again, I smashed right into Coach Hollylighter. She looked at me for a second like she wasn't sure what I was doing there, even though she'd just read my name.

"I just wanted to say thanks for giving me a chance," I told her, fumbling over the words.

She nodded with none of yesterday's smiles. "Sure," she said. "We needed a good fill-in and I know you were Luther's star. So let's see if you can."

Let's see? Really, would it kill her to say "I know you can do it!"? But maybe she was nervous. And maybe not every coach I met was going to be exactly how I wanted them to be.

We took the field first. And the sensation I had on the mound was nothing like my jinx game. Maybe it was because I was thinking about winning differently, but I didn't have all that knotty energy bundled up in my belly. I just felt right.

In the first inning, I pitched to three batters—the top of the batting order—and struck them all out. My arm was on fire, in a good way.

We didn't score any runs but I held the score to zero in the second inning—still with no one on base!—and then Mario drove in Ryder for our first run.

1–0.

I'm not sure if it was the good feelings I had, or because I missed playing so much, or if it was because I wanted to show the team I was worth having around, but I kept throwing stuff like I couldn't miss. So all the Firecrackers batters could do was miss.

And by the sixth inning, I was on track for a no-hitter. My third unicorn of the year and my first as a Penguin!!!

In the dugout before our at bat, Mario handed me a cup of water from the cooler. "Great game . . . Gabby." Not *Gaggy*.

I squinted at him and looked

at the water to see if his fingernail clippings were floating in it.

It looked like plain old water.

"Did you spit in this?"

"No. But I guess what I'm trying to say is, if you're going to be pitching, I'm glad it's to my opponent and not to me."

I took a cautious sip. It tasted like normal water. "Well, thanks, Mario."

He rolled his eyes. "Don't get used to it. Just, you know, get us the win."

I had a feeling I would—in the last inning, we'd scored several runs and were up 5–0—but I wasn't getting that excited "I'm gonna win!" feeling. I wasn't unhappy, at all, but my energy was somewhere else.

Another epiphany struck.

I thought that maybe I wasn't so afraid of failing this time because my mind was on the talent showcase. I was wondering how my friends were doing. I wanted to cheer them on.

But then I realized there was a second true-to-me thing I had to be, besides a baseball player: a friend. Epiphanies were really hard to schedule! But I couldn't ignore it.

"Coach, I think you should put in a reliever," I said suddenly to Coach Hollylighter. I just blurted it out like that.

She raised an eyebrow. "Is something wrong? Your arm looks great."

It was the nicest thing she'd ever said to me. And it was

true. I was on the verge of a **UNICORN**.

It was hard to say the words, but I did: "It feels great, but there's another team that needs me."

Coach Hollylighter stared at me so long that I wondered if she was Devon's opposite: a non-blinker.

"Hmm," she said. "I think I understand. I think you're making the right choice, and I respect it. And you got us a nice lead. Great game, Garcia. Go get 'em." Multiple compliments! Whoa. And she patted my shoulder supportively!

"Thanks, Coach!" I yelled, already on my way to the bleachers where, before I said a word, Louie piped up.

"Do you want us to stay here or go with you?" My dad had filled her in the night before and now she must have been reading my mind. ESP finally worked!

"You stay and cheer them on," I said. "I just know where I need to be now."

I stopped for a second and looked from Louie to my dad. "Or should I stay?"

My dad smiled. "When you can't do everything, you do what you can."

I knew he was right and I just hoped there was time.

Johnny jogged up alongside me as I headed off the field. For such an academic guy, he could really run. Even in a tie. "What are you doing? This is one of the best games in school history!"

"It is?" Of course it was. It was a unicorn—what was I thinking? How many unicorns did a school get in its life?

But there were things more magical than unicorns. The talent squad had welcomed me just for being me. Or at least the me I was pretending to be. They encouraged my poetry, even when it was bad, and they appreciated me even when no one else seemed to. It seemed wrong to let them down when I didn't have to.

"Yeah, the game is awesome," Johnny said. "I knew you were great. I mean, are great. Would be great . . ."

He looked down at his shoes like he was embarrassed, even though he was saying such nice things.

"Thanks for, um, thanks for . . ." I didn't know how to say what I wanted to. "Thanks for pestering me all the time about playing baseball."

He shrugged. "I like good statistics."

"I'm not mad or anything, but why did you push Coach H. to get me to sub in for Devon when you knew I had the talent showcase?"

His face turned as red as his Piper Bell Penguins tie.

Now he looked up at me and even if I told myself I didn't have a crush, I thought maybe I could have a hypothetical one. "I just thought if anyone could handle it, it was you."

Or not hypothetical.

The "thank you" I said came out like a dribble of weird syllables.

"You should go," Johnny said. "There's still time."

I made it to the backstage area just before the show started.

Howell Jefferson, the student body president, was onstage at the podium while three different cameras filmed him. There were also people in the audience with signs and banners for some of the performers—I saw people who, based on their banners, I guessed were Katy's relatives, and Molly's, and Sophia's.

I ducked backstage, feeling sweaty from the game. Or maybe from nerves. Or both.

Molly was the first person to see me. Probably because she's taller than anyone else.

"Gabby?" Everyone turned to look at me, and I was surprised that they all looked happy to see me.

"I came to see you guys," I said, and wondered how grubby and crazy I looked since I was just on the mound and also seconds ago discovered I had my first crush. I kept hearing Johnny say, "I just thought if anyone could handle it, it was you."

The poetic term for what I was feeling is **SWOON**.

"But you left us the poems. And those bomb cookies," Sophia said.

"We were kind of hard on you yesterday," Katy said. "And you're not that bad of a poet. I mean, you need work, that's for sure, but nothing hanging out with me can't fix."

"Katy!" Molly said, and I thought she'd be mad at Katy for bragging but then she said, "I'm the real writer here, so come on! I'll teach Gabby what she needs to know."

Everyone started debating—but in a nice way—who was going to make me into a stellar poet, and just like that, I felt good again. Maybe I would even become a great poet.

But then we heard Howell introduce Katy as a singing-dancing-songwriting dynamo.

"Well, I guess it's time for us to go win this thing, ya think?" Katy shook out her arms and legs and grinned at us. "Glad our good luck charm made it!" She blew me a kiss as she and her dancers ran out onstage.

See the day
Rise to meet it
Every start is a fresh one
And we're gonna get it

The lights and the booming sound made me feel like we weren't in the school auditorium but at the halftime show of the Super Bowl. Beyoncé would have been impressed.

If I have to predict the future, I'm pretty sure that Katy

will be singing the national anthem at the World Series game I pitch in.

The applause was huge and when Katy returned backstage, she threw her arms around me. "We're gonna win this thing!" she said, looking at the computer monitor backstage that showed the votes coming in. One act in, we had the most of the four schools. By a lot.

Then Molly read from her book and the audience was in tears. People voting must have been equally into the book, because the total votes rose again! Was I really a good luck charm? Nah, I thought. My friends are just super-talented.

Molly looked at the monitor in disbelief. "We might get to go to New York. OMG." It's a big deal for her to say that, as she doesn't like abbreviations.

She smiled at me. "I'm sorry I said such mean things about your poetry," she told me. "I can't believe you wrote all those haikus."

I smiled back. "It's okay," I said. "It was wrong of me to lie. I should have just asked you guys to help me find a talent, or told you what happened with the baseball team."

"People don't always say or do what they should. There'd be a lot less to write about if they did," Molly said. "So did you win?"

I shook my head. "No idea."

"What?? How do you not know? G, you better spill," Katy said with a hand on her hip.

"I left so I could come here," I said. There was also one other thing, a secret I'd almost been keeping from myself. I really **DID** want to perform in the talent showcase. And for the first time, I had a poem I thought was the real deal. I'd written it the night before. "Also, I was hoping to read a new thing I wrote." I wouldn't have asked if the team was still mad at me, but since they weren't, I felt ready to take the stage.

Sophia grabbed me by the shoulders. "You have to go back to the game, though."

Molly nodded. "Yeah, you shouldn't be here. We can't ruin this for you."

"I took myself out of the game," I said. "I wanted to be here." I pulled the folded-up poem from inside my jersey. "Plus, this."

Coach Raddock stepped forward. "Here's what we're going to do," she said, sounding just like a coach in a movie at a key dramatic moment. "You're going to read that, and then you're getting back on that baseball field."

She was right. Because as I thought about Devon and Bobby and even Mario, I didn't want to let them down either. I was out as pitcher. Once a pitcher came out, that was that. But I could help in some other way.

WHY, OH WHY, COULDN'T I BE EVERYWHERE AT ONCE?

As Arlo finished his rousing speech and the monitor showed our votes tick up again, Coach Raddock nudged me out onto the stage.

I wasn't quite ready. I was still sweaty and red-faced and I'd only read the poem in my bedroom. Actually, I'd only read it under my covers, right before I fell asleep. But as the audience looked up at me expectantly, and Katy whispered, "Read!" from her place in the wings, I found my voice.

The thrill of victory
Is too big to rhyme

271

With anything
Because it's not just some word
It's not even a thing at all
Victory is everything along the way
You pick up the ball
And you throw
And it goes goes goes
And when the batter swings
They can't touch it
And that's one little piece of victory
When the crowd claps for your team
That's part of the win
You feel it rise up through your mitt
Into your arms
It slips beneath your cap
Into your head
And slides through the button of your jersey
Into your heart
So it's not just a scoring play
Or a W on your stats
Or even your team carrying you off the field
It's knowing you did things
Exactly right
It's knowing you didn't
Let anyone down

And the day
Belongs to you
And that's too big to rhyme
With anything

And then the audience clapped. And cheered. And gave me a win.

It was good. My poem was good! But better than good, it was honest. I was crying a little but I pretended it was sweat.

"That kicked butt," Katy said. "**THAT** was your poem! But now you have to go back, G!" She was already pulling me by the elbow off the stage.

"It might be over by now."

"Well, you have to find out, don't you?" Molly joined us on my other side and pulled me along too. "You wouldn't let us miss *our* chances at greatness."

Back outside, it was like we had an unspoken agreement to make a mad dash for the field.

That ESP really was coming through all over the place.

And the game was not over. Far from it. It was the top of the ninth. Lailah was having an awful inning. There were players on every base. The Firecrackers had scored a couple runs, too, so it was 5–2.

Johnny, who was standing behind the backstop, looked up at us and grimaced. "You're back." He paused. "Things are bad. She did okay after you left until a few minutes ago. She needs to get someone out. They could tie the score with one decent hit."

As if he was getting advice from Johnny, the batter at the plate swung big and hit a nice shot to right field. Madeleine was jogging for it, she was under it, her glove was out.

And then she smashed into the outfield wall.

Yup.

Nose first.

At least this time there was no blood. She threw the ball toward home, but the batter drove in three runs. The score was tied. And the batter made it to third—scoring position. And *then* Madeleine's nose started to bleed.

At least I wasn't responsible.

(Though maybe it wouldn't have happened if I hadn't left the game.)

I ran to the dugout as Coach Hollylighter called for a time-out so she could pull Madeleine.

She looked surprised when she saw me, and even more surprised when she saw Molly and Katy run up behind me.

"You came back?" she asked.

I couldn't tell from her expression if she was happy about it or not.

"I know," I said. "I'm sorry I left. I shouldn't have done that."

She looked at my friends behind me. "You had to support

both your teams," she said. "Do you think you can take over in right field? And Madeleine's spot in the batting order?"

Madeleine, who was holding an ice pack to her nose, nodded. "Yeah, there's no way I'm going back out there," she said. "Maybe ever."

I hate playing right field. No one really wants to play right field, because nothing ever happens in right field. Or hardly ever.

Well, unless you're Madeleine, I guess, but what happened to her is hardly good.

"Sure," I said.

I pulled on my mitt and headed for right, trying to get my bearings for this spot on the field. I was proud of myself. Old Gabby would have been embarrassed to go from pitching a unicorn to standing in right field.

Lailah was pitching to a left-handed batter. Left-handed batters often hit to right field. And the batter smashed the ball on Lailah's first pitch. The ball was a fast-moving grounder and it was coming my way.

I dropped down to field the ball but bobbled it a little. Ugh. I steadied myself, grabbed the ball, and hurled it to home. But it wasn't enough. The third-base runner hustled and slid on his stomach just as my throw reached Ryder's glove.

"Safe!" the ump yelled.

Franklin was up 6–5.

Another thing that was my fault.

Coach Hollylighter pulled Lailah and put in Casey Dotson, a reliever who hadn't played much this season. We were at the weak spot of the Franklin batting order and Casey managed the out.

But the inning had left the team shaken.

Bob: *Did Gabby make the worst mistake ever by leaving this game?*

Judy: *Bob, if I knew the answer to that question, Gabby wouldn't need to keep both of us around.*

So we were only down one run, but that was a big deal. A bad inning could destroy a team. One bad inning on the field could turn a whole good game into a roller coaster ride of doom. And right now, the Penguins looked like they were on that coaster and like every last one of them was going to be sick.

In fast-moving sports like football or basketball, all the running and moving means every second could be a drama. In baseball, the story unfolds slowly sometimes. Things could go really great for a long time, but just when it seems like the game is going to one team, a bad break could mean everything gets messy.

It's one of the best and worst things about the game.

Coach Hollylighter was trying her best at a pep talk, but she was having a hard time. She was nervous, too, because we were starting the inning at the bottom of the batting order with Samuel Jinkins and now Casey Dotson. No one wanted to tell the weak batters that they were the weak spot, but they knew it too.

We were all silent as Samuel and Casey took their at bats.

And both struck out.

We were back at the top of the order, but things could go either way. But then Ryder hit a line drive to center and hustled to first. Danny Pettuci managed a walk. We had runners on first and second.

And I was up in Madeleine's spot.

Goal: Win the game.

Action: A home run to drive in Ryder and Danny. And me.

I could see it now.

Movie-Moment Gabby, saving the day.

My whole body was tingling. I could fix everything, make everyone happy, with one big hit.

At the plate, I stared coolly at the pitcher.

The first pitch was a fastball, right in the strike zone. I swung huge, thinking **GOGOGOGOGOGO**, hoping the ball could hear me.

I missed.

The second pitch . . . same thing. I looked at the outfield wall, imagining my hit soaring over it, and everyone celebrating **ME**.

SCREECH! My mind halted the daydream. I was still trying to make things perfect and **WIN** everything all by myself.

If I kept swinging like this, I was going to strike out.

I thought about what my dad said and what Johnny said and what Diego said.

If you can't do everything, you do what you can.

I just thought if anyone could handle it, it would be you.

It's not a weakness to just say what you want sometimes.

I knew what I needed to do. I needed to **NOT** try to hit a home run.

Small ball.

Small ball.

It wasn't about the home run.

It wasn't about me.

It wasn't about the perfect thing happening.

I just needed to get on base.

When the pitcher let go of the ball again, I swung, but not like I was trying to crush the ball into a million pieces. Instead, I did what I could.

CRACK!

And the hit was good, a low-flying ball between center and left field.

I ran as fast as I could to first. Ryder and Danny sprinted to the next base. Bases were loaded. And Mario was up.

He looked like he was going to be sick. And I was going to ask him, of all people, for what I wanted.

"You can do this," I shouted to him from my place on first as he left the dugout, taking a few lackluster swings on his way to the plate.

He turned. "And if I can't, we're done."

"You can. Pretend the pitcher is me."

"What? No way. That's a horrible idea." Now he looked genuinely scared.

I shook my head. "You're **DUE** to get a hit off me. I know it. So pretend this is your hit off me."

"You're crazy, Garcia," he said. "But I'll try it."

By now, I could see more of the talent squad in the stands. And they looked happy. I already had a feeling that I knew why. But I had to keep my head in this game for now. Everyone was on their feet on both the Penguins' side and the Firecrackers' side.

YEP, MARIO TOTALLY THINKS I'M CUCKOO...

Bases were loaded and Mario was our best batter.

This had just gone from small ball to possibly big-deal ball.

I think I stopped breathing as the pitcher threw a curve and Mario swung. And missed.

GABBY & MARIO
TEAMMATES FOR REAL ?

BOB   JUDY

≡ INSIDE GABBY'S BRAIN ≡

Bob: Did you ever think Gabby Garcia would be hoping Mario Salamida would get a grand slam?

Judy: Bob, I think we've learned that we can't predict anything!

The umpire called the next two pitches balls. The fluttery feeling in my stomach moved up into my chest. Could we win on a walk?

But on the next pitch, Mario swung. It wasn't going to be a grand slam, though. The ball was a grounder that wasn't going to make it out of the infield. It was not the hit we needed.

But, over or not, the bases were loaded and we had to run anyway.

So we did.

The ball was rolling right for me and the second baseman was looking to get it.

I hopped over it and then threw myself into a slide to second.

I peeked through the dust around me and saw Ryder crossing home and Danny rounding third and heading there. But if I was out first, Danny's run wouldn't count.

I touched the base with my fingertips a split second before the second baseman reached it.

"Safe!" the ump yelled.

SAFE! SAFE! SAFE!

We'd won, 7–6!

"We're going to regionals!" Coach Hollylighter yelped, louder than I'd ever heard her say anything. She ran onto the field, smiling for maybe the first time in her life. The rest of the team was behind her, beaming.

I pitched us into regionals! Or, okay, I partly pitched us into regionals. And then I hit us into regionals. Or kind of did. And then I pep-talked us into regionals. Sort of.

No, **WE**—the Penguins—got us into regionals.

REGIONALS!

The field was a mess of people. The baseball team hugged and high-fived. Madeleine seemed to forget her nose problems and dropped her ice pack to spin around with Devon. Mario was fist-bumping everyone in sight and Ryder Mills's whole family had him locked in the center of a hug. Molly and Katy were talking to my parents.

And I heard them say something about my poem. And **NEW YORK**.

NEW YORK and **REGIONALS**???

Please, don't let them be the same day, I thought.

Nope, I was celebrating everything and not going to let what might happen next ruin anything

Then someone tapped me on the shoulder and I turned around to see . . .

Johnny Madden.

I swear his eyes had gotten greener over the last few innings. I didn't think this day could get better!

"That was a great game," he said. "I mean, I thought it would be."

Whatever calm feelings I had today were gone because I had the new, not-calm feelings of perhaps, maybe, having a crush.

Bob: *Whoa, Judy, this is brand-new territory for Garcia.*

Judy: *But Bob, how great is her day going? She's got her friends back,*

she's got the win, and Johnny Madden is probably crushing on her right back. Plus, she's headed to regionals!

Bob: And New York! What a win streak! Piper Bell Academy was a solid move for Garcia, it seems. To think she wanted to go back to Luther.

Yeah, Bob, I thought. My win streak was back, I couldn't help but agree. And I felt like I was right where I belonged more than I ever had in my life. Weird, crush-having, barfy feeling aside.

Because the Bob-and-Judy comments were filling up my brain, I was having a hard time responding to Johnny.

"Thanks," I said. "I can't believe we'll be going to regionals. And New York, for the talent squad. I'm freaking out."

Now Johnny frowned. "Wait, so you didn't hear?"

"Hear what?" Oh no, regionals and the New York trip were going to be the same weekend. Well, I'd figure it out.

"Luther's asbestos-free. It's reopening for the last few weeks of the school year. Won't you go back there?"

What?

WHAT?

So now I was going to regionals, and to New York, **AND** back to Luther???

It sounds like I'll need some new plays for sure!

ACKNOWLEDGMENTS

In writing a book, it would be nice to somehow include a play-by-play of all the ways people help along the way, through encouragement, understanding, letting me read things aloud in a neurotic way, calm guidance when I feel like nothing's working, and the occasional caffeinated provisions. I guess the closest thing I have is acknowledgments, so here goes.

Big, huge, scoreboard-lighting-up-and-fireworks-exploding thank-yous to:

Claudia Gabel, editor extraordinaire, for her energy, patience, and guidance in helping me bring Gabby and her friends to the page. Thanks for fielding my questions (and my puns) and wonderfully coaching me as I rounded the bases of bringing a book into the world.

Marta Kissi for making me *squee* with delight at her illustrations of Gabby and company, and to Amy Ryan and

Katie Fitch for their art and design know-how.

Alex Arnold and Maria Barbo Editora, who tossed me some great notes and pitched some excellent ideas for early stages of this book.

Katherine Tegen and the entire team at Katherine Tegen Books for supporting this project. Special mentions to Rebecca Aronson and Emily Rader for keeping things moving, and to Meaghan Finnerty for getting Gabby in front of the right crowds.

My agent, Fonda Snyder, who so frequently cheers me on when I need it, and who always makes me feel like I'm hitting it out of the park.

My dad and mom, Bill and Debra Palmer, who came to all my games and cheered me on, even on the days when I mostly daydreamed in the outfield. (And for always knowing I was more writer than an athlete.) I'm a very lucky daughter.

My sons, Clark and Nathan Stanis, who, if I'm being totally honest, have a capacity for distraction and destruction that was in no way helpful to finishing any of the drafts of this book but who light up my heart each and every day, no matter how chaotic things get.

My husband, Steve Stanis, who catches whatever I throw at him . . . . even me. I love you so much.